For Frank, spending Christmas Eve with Amy is better than any dream.

Frank needed both hands to turn Gray and the sleigh back toward town. Then he urged Gray to a stop. He slid his arm back around Amy's shoulders and risked pulling her close in a gentle hug. Wonder wrapped around his heart at the trusting way she relaxed into his embrace.

He breathed in the sweet scent that lingered about her soft hair, then touched his lips to her neck, at that place just below the dainty, purple stones that dangled from her ear. He drew his head back slightly and, barely breathing, kissed her lips. "Amy, you are so precious," he whispered, then met her warm lips again. She surrendered a kiss so sweet his chest ached.

And finally he kissed the snowflakes off her lashes.

"We'd better get home," he repeated.

Amy's head rested against his shoulder as he drove. To Frank it seemed love enclosed them in a circle so strong it was tangible.

JOANN A. GROTE lives in Minnesota where she grew up. She uses the state for most of her story settings, and like her characters, JoAnn seeks to serve Christ in her work. She believes that readers of novels can receive a message of salvation and encouragement from well-crafted fiction. She has had several novels published with Barbour Publishing in the **Heartsong Presents** line as well as in the *American Adventure* series for kids.

HEARTSONG PRESENTS

Books by JoAnn A. Grote
HP36—The Sure Promise
HP51—The Unfolding Heart
HP55—Treasure of the Heart
HP103—Love's Shining Hope
HP120—An Honest Love
HP136—Rekindled Flame
HP184—Hope That Sings
HP288—Sweet Surrender
HP331—A Man for Libby
HP377—Come Home to My Heart

Don't miss out on any of our super romances. Write to us at the following address for information on our newest releases and club membership.

Heartsong Presents Readers' Service
PO Box 721
Uhrichsville, OH 44683

Or visit us at www.heartsongpresents.com

Hold on
My Heart

JoAnn A. Grote

Heartsong Presents

To Kristy, Gideon's guardian angel

A note from the author:
*I love to hear from my readers! You may correspond with me
by writing:*

> **JoAnn A. Grote**
> **Author Relations**
> **PO Box 719**
> **Uhrichsville, OH 44683**

ISBN 1-58660-527-5

HOLD ON MY HEART

All Scripture quotations, unless otherwise noted, are taken from
the King James Version of the Bible.

All of the characters and events in this book are fictitious. Any
resemblance to actual persons, living or dead, or to actual events
is purely coincidental.

Cover design by Nancy White Cassidy.

PRINTED IN THE U.S.A.

one

Chippewa City, Minnesota—1894

Entering the large room, Frank Sterling immediately began searching for Amy Henderson. He acknowledged greetings from friends as he moved through the crowd of Windom Academy students but didn't allow them to distract him from his goal. Floral scents from young ladies' colognes mixed with Bay Rum aftershave popular with the male students, and both blended with the spicy pine branches, which decorated the academy hall for the Christmas party. No cigar smoke clouded the air; the students wouldn't take the chance of losing their cherished place at the Academy by breaking the smoking rule.

A female classmate at the refreshment table offered him a cup of hot apple cider rich with cinnamon, and he flashed her a smile as he accepted it. "Thanks." She giggled and blushed in response and looked away in apparent embarrassment. He found her girlishness annoying. Amy never acted immature like so many of the girls their age.

Just at that moment, he found her. He lowered his cup and drank in the sight of her.

She sat on a simple oak chair in a corner of the room, straight and tall with her usual gentle dignity. A white-globed kerosene lamp on the lace-covered oak table beside her cast light on the sketch pad in her lap and brought out the glimmers of gold in her brown hair, which swept in graceful waves to the top of her head.

Walter Bay, the man she was sketching, stood with one hand

beneath his coat in a poor imitation of Napoleon's famous pose. Frank felt his lips tighten in distaste. Mr. Bay must be thirty if he was a day, half again as old as Frank and Amy and the other Academy students. Bay preferred to be called Professor, but everyone at the school knew he hadn't earned the title. He had a university education and was a successful businessman. It was for those reasons he taught courses in economics. Frank had no time for the man. "Thinks the sun can't rise without his help," Frank had told his brother, Jason.

He ran a finger beneath his starched white collar. It was mighty uncomfortable compared to the work clothes he'd broken in with his daily farm chores. Seemed he couldn't grow accustomed to wearing the scratchy collars, even though he'd been wearing them for the entire fall semester.

Amy glanced up and caught Frank watching her. Did her smile deepen, her gray eyes brighten a bit in gladness at seeing him, or was it imagination? He chose to believe what his heart affirmed. Pleasure scrolled through him.

Frank felt someone nudge him and turned. "Hi, Roland."

His blond classmate was a year older than Frank and tended toward roundness, where Frank's slim frame was muscular from years of farm chores.

"Want something stronger than that apple cider?" Roland winked and nudged Frank again. "A bunch of us are getting together later at Bjorg's place."

"No, thanks."

"Are you sure? It's a cold night. Could use something to warm you before heading back to your farm."

"I'm sure. Better be careful. If you get caught, you won't be coming back after the holiday."

"We know the rules. We aren't so stupid as to get caught," Roland blustered. "If you change your mind about joining us, let me know."

Frank was glad when Roland walked away. He turned his

attention back to Amy. She was engrossed in her drawing, her hand moving with sure, quick strokes. He smiled. Go drinking? Not a chance. A year ago when he'd asked Amy to court him, her father had made it clear he'd only allow Frank to keep company with his daughter if Frank went a year without drinking or gambling.

The memory of Mr. Henderson telling Frank he wasn't worthy of Amy always embarrassed Frank and made him want to reach for the bottle he'd promised not to touch. He realized now in surprise that the memory no longer left him uncomfortable. He felt proud and strong because he'd kept his promise.

Amy had assured him that she knew he'd keep his word and that to celebrate they'd attend Christmas Eve services together. At first a year had sounded like forever. He'd strengthened his resolve by recalling the Old Testament story of Jacob's fourteen-year wait for Rachel. Jacob's wait had been longer, but Jacob hadn't had to give up drinking.

At times during the last year, Frank had almost given in and reached for a bottle. Like after a hot, sticky, dirty day on the farm, when even the night didn't bring a refreshing breeze to cool the air, and a cold beer sounded like manna from heaven. Or worse, when he saw some other man escort Amy to a dance and knew he himself hadn't the right to ask for even one dance. Amy was well worth the price of giving up drinking and gambling.

Though he and Amy hadn't discussed the situation since last December, whenever their gazes met, her eyes had shined with faith in him. Or had he only imagined it?

His year of testing would be up next week. He'd kept his promise. Would Amy keep hers?

❧

Amy handed Walter the sketch. "There you are, Mr. Bay."

He didn't take the paper from her as she expected. Instead, he leaned over the drawing, leaving it in her hand. The nearness of his cheek so close to hers awakened an unpleasant desire within her to flee. Flight was impossible, even it weren't rude. He blocked her only way of escape.

"Lovely, Miss Henderson."

He wasn't looking at the paper. He was looking into her eyes. She drew her head back and set the drawing on the table, removing his excuse for closeness. "I'm glad you like it." Her voice sounded stiffer than the dead pine needles in the decorations about the room. "I hope you'll think it worthy of a donation for the Academy." She indicated the crystal bowl, which already held a smattering of coins.

He straightened, chuckling, and drew a few coins from his pocket. "Well worth the price."

The expression in his eyes left no doubt that it was the improper closeness he believed worth the price. Amy felt herself withdrawing. Her spine pressed against the back of the chair.

A small man with a beard touched Bay's arm. "Ah, Mr. Bay, just the man I need."

Amy let out a soft sigh of relief at Professor Headley's arrival.

"Mrs. Headley and I were discussing where to hold our astronomy class next semester," the professor continued. "Would you join us at our table?"

"Of course." Walter picked up the sketch as Headley drew him away. "I was just complimenting Miss Henderson on the sketch she drew of me."

Headley darted an apologetic look over his shoulder at Amy. She hoped he understood the message of gratitude in her own eyes for his intervention.

Headley settled his hand on Bay's shoulder. "We're fortunate she offered to use her talent to raise money for us. There are never enough funds for all the Academy's needs, as you well know. About that astronomy class. . ."

Their voices faded as they moved away. Amy let her gaze drift back to where she'd last seen Frank. For the first time that evening, none of the students or faculty were sitting for her. She'd hoped Frank would take advantage of her freedom and come over, but he was visiting with members of the football team.

Her disappointment melted into delight. It was a wonderful opportunity to sketch Frank without appearing to single him out. She had sketches of him at home, but they'd all been done from memory. Her hand raced over the page, capturing the three young men in earnest conversation. She was finishing the drawing when Frank broke away from the others. A minute later he was walking toward her with a cup of cider in each hand. Her heart quickened its beat, as it always did when he was near.

"I thought you might be thirsty, Miss Amy."

"How thoughtful." She accepted with a smile the cup he offered. For a moment she considered turning her sketchbook so he wouldn't see what she'd drawn, then decided it would appear more innocent if she didn't hide it.

"Nice party. A good send-off for the students who will be traveling a distance home for the holidays."

"Yes." The look in his eyes held a compliment which propriety didn't allow him to express since they weren't courting. Amy felt herself flush with pleasure. She was glad she'd worn her new silk trimmed with velvet, which brought out the green in her gray-green eyes.

"The girls did a wonderful job decorating the hall considering how little they had to spend, don't you think?" Amy asked to fill the emotion-packed silence that had fallen between them. "They spent hours and hours making the paper roses. I understand someone donated a barrel of evergreen boughs."

"Walter Bay donated them."

"Oh."

He grinned. "Maybe we should start a pine-planting tradition so one day the town won't need to import pine trees and boughs for Christmas. When the original settlers started this prairie town twenty or so years ago, there were trees only along the river, and now elms shade every house and street. No telling how twenty years of pine planting would change the land."

"It sounds like a wonderful idea." The part that sounded most wonderful to her was the "we" in his plan. If only it weren't simply a manner of speech.

Please let him ask me to the Christmas Eve service, Amy prayed silently. She'd waited all evening, hoping for these few precious minutes with him, hoping he would take the opportunity to ask her to the service. She tried to maintain an illusion of calm and proper womanly decorum, but inside she felt she would burst from anticipation.

A trill of piano keys quieted the crowd and brought everyone's attention to the corner opposite Amy and Frank. Young Mrs. Headley invited everyone to gather around the piano for a group sing. A violinist joined the pianist in playing "O Little Town of Bethlehem." The crowd raised their voices in song as they drifted toward the musicians.

Frank held out his hand to Amy. "Shall we join them?"

She placed her hand in his willingly and rose. His hand was calloused but his touch firm and gentle. She was disappointed when he let go of her hand after giving her fingers a quick, soft squeeze. *What did you expect?* she chided herself as they crossed the room. She knew the answer. She'd not expected, but hoped, he would offer her his arm. Couples in the early stages of courting, scattered through the crowd, stood together with the woman's hand snuggled in the crook of the gentleman's arm. It was perfectly acceptable behavior for unengaged couples.

She should have known Frank wouldn't draw her hand

through his arm. Likely he considered it a liberty not allowed since he had promised her father he wouldn't court her for a year.

Frank's bass resonated beside her as he joined in the singing, sending delight rippling through her. How silly to waste this special time wishing for more when they stood together celebrating Christ's birth. She caught the melody in her soprano voice. She glanced up at him and saw his eyes smiling into hers.

As the song ended, Amy heard Walter whisper, "You have a beautiful singing voice, Miss Amy."

She jumped slightly. The hair on the back of her neck rose in a chill of surprise. She hadn't realized he stood beside her. Her murmured "thank you" wasn't heartfelt.

After each song Walter made some trifling comment to her. Normally Amy wouldn't have found this annoying, but tonight he felt like an intruder. His constant attentions prevented Frank from taking the opportunity to speak to her even casually, let alone to extend the Christmas Eve invitation she'd been waiting for all year.

Was it her imagination, or was Frank withdrawing from her as the hymn sing progressed? Did Frank think she welcomed Walter's attentions? What could she do about it without appearing rude?

After a half-dozen songs, the students took a break in their singing to present their gifts to Professor and Mrs. Headley. The young couple's devotion to the school endeared them to their pupils. Light from the kerosene lamp atop the piano reflected off tears in Mrs. Headley's eyes when she pulled from the round, blue-papered box a small hat with two pheasant feathers perkily peeking up from the back. Amy blinked back her own tears. She'd selected the gift, but it was from all the students. She'd seen Mrs. Headley's gaze linger on the adorable hat in Miss Hermanson's millinery window when they were shopping together. Mrs. Headley never spoke of the small luxuries she neglected to purchase for herself, but it was common knowledge in the village that the luxuries were willingly passed over in exchange for spending much of her husband's salary on school necessities.

Professor Headley's gift of sturdy bib overalls from the students brought laughter from all. The young man had accepted the headship of the fledgling private school, understanding his duties to include distributing the budget. He soon discovered the budget didn't provide money in these hard times following the Panic of '93 for someone to dig the well, or build the footbridge over the deep, tree-filled gully between the school and town, or any of the other numerous acts of physical labor necessary. He dove into the acts himself without complaint, but they were a hardship on his clothes, which were not suited to such labor. His mended, worn trousers and shirts were quiet testimony to the students that he hadn't money to spare on new outfits. The overalls would protect what good clothing he had left.

"That was an appropriate send-off," Frank said with a chuckle after the last lines of the last tune, "God Rest Ye, Merry Gentlemen."

"Yes." Amy smiled up at him. If he were going to ask her to the Christmas Eve service, surely he would do so now. Could he understand the encouragement she tried to send with her expression? Already chattering students were retrieving their coats. In only a moment the opportunity might be gone.

"May I see you home, Miss Amy?"

Walter's offer shattered her hopes. Frank's eyes darkened, and his face looked as though he'd pulled a drapery across it, hiding his emotions. Amy wanted to stamp her feet in tantrum like a three year old. Decorum allowed no such display.

"Thank you for offering, Mr. Bay, but that won't be necessary. Some of us who live in town are walking home together." She was relieved the arrangement gave her an excuse to decline.

Sylvia, the blond, petite girl who had served the cider, stopped beside them. "Here's your coat, Amy. The others are ready to leave." As always, her words tumbled after each other in a breathless rush.

Frank held Amy's coat for her. She wondered what it would feel like if his arms wrapped around her. Would they be as warm and comforting in life's storms as her coat against winter's harsh winds?

Sylvia flashed her smile at Frank and then Walter. Her blue eyes shone. "Would you gentlemen like to join us? We have quite a nice-sized group." She waved a gloved hand toward the door where a half-dozen men and women were gathered. "The more the merrier."

Walter accepted immediately. Frank hesitated a moment before saying, "Sure. It sounds like fun."

The anticipation of more time near Frank thrilled Amy. She'd have preferred Walter not join them, but after all, it was a large group. Surely he wouldn't expect her attention to be addressed to him.

Most likely Frank's horse was at the Academy. He'd need to return from the residential section to retrieve the horse. Certainly that indicated he wanted to spend more time with her, didn't it? Or perhaps, her more cautionary side whispered, he only wanted to spend more time with the rest of their jolly friends before returning home to the quiet of the farmhouse.

The evening was lovely, with barely a breeze. Snowflakes drifted lazily in the pale yellow light cast on the snow-covered ground by the lanterns on either side of the front door. Frank and Walter were on each side of Amy as they descended the stairs. At the bottom of the stairs, Frank fell in beside her. The shoveled path was not wide enough for more than two people.

Amy caught the glance of annoyance Walter darted at Frank before dropping back to walk beside Sylvia.

Amy turned up the large collar of her gray wool coat. The maroon velvet trim felt soft and warm against her ears, and she was grateful for it. Her hat was a fashionable affair not designed to keep one warm. Her plush maroon muffler secured the collar in place.

A couple of the boys carried lanterns. The shadows of the troupe lengthened and shortened against the snow as the lanterns swung. There were no other buildings on the prairie on the village's edge, no streetlights or stray beams from parlors to help guide their way beneath the cloud-covered sky, but they were all familiar with the path across the former field.

The light had been lit at the narrow walking bridge over the gully between the Windom land and the town. Amy could see snow dapple the brims of the men's hats and the shoulders of everyone's coats. Snow dusted the bridge planks, sparkling in the flickering light as though set with diamonds. "Careful, the bridge is slippery," one of the first to cross called back.

Amy reached for the wooden handrail when she stepped onto the bridge. She felt the slight pressure of Frank's hand at her lower back and was grateful for it. By the time they reached the middle of the bridge, she walked with confidence. Amy glanced over her shoulder at Frank. "It's not too slippery. Oooh!"

Her feet flew out from under her. She fell backward, her descent stopped suddenly when Frank's strong arms closed around her. Her head collided with his chest, and she felt her hat fall free of its hat pin. Frank's heart beat fast and strong against her back, even through their heavy winter coats.

"I have you, Amy." His breath was warm against her cheek. She barely had time to register the fact before he was helping her regain her footing. "Steady now," he whispered against her hair. He guided her gently away from the side of the bridge, moving himself between her and the railing. One arm still around her waist, he looked down into the gulch. "Looks like you've lost your hat."

Everyone was watching her, all asking at once whether she was all right or warning too late to be careful. Sylvia was giggling as usual. "You've lost your topknot, too, Amy."

Her gloved hands brushed at her hair, though she knew it was useless. The carefully pinned bun had slid from the top of her head to her neck, just behind one ear. It would probably have fallen farther if not for her jacket's high collar.

"Are you sure you weren't harmed, Miss Amy?" Concern filled Frank's question. "Did you wrench your ankle?"

"No, I'm fine. All that are hurt are my pride and my hat." She sighed slightly. "I only purchased that hat yesterday, and I did fancy it."

The near-fall had happened so quickly that Amy hadn't had time to be frightened. Now she realized she could have tumbled through the snowy night into the gulch along with her hat. She shoved suddenly shaking hands into her maroon muff. "Thank you, Frank." Her voice shook as badly as her hands. Taking a deep breath, she stepped carefully forward.

Frank's hand slipped from her back. She regretted it, missing the sense of safety, but a moment later he offered his arm. She took it, welcoming the safety back.

She was pleasantly surprised that he didn't remove his arm when they reached the path on the opposite side of the gulch. Did he allow her hand to remain snug within the bend of his elbow in case of another unexpectedly slippery path or because he enjoyed the closeness? She hoped the latter.

Yet if he still cared, why hadn't he asked her to the Christmas Eve service? In the midst of the group's bright conversation, her mind wandered over the last year.

Amy hadn't seen Frank with any other girls, not once.

Chippewa City was so small that one always heard if anyone was courting, and sometimes even when they weren't, the rumor mill carried the question of maybe so. She was sure her school friends would pass the tidbit of her and Frank walking home hand-in-arm about town by this time tomorrow.

Even if Frank had managed to spend time with another young woman without the town discovering it, his sister-in-law, Pearl, would have seen it, Amy knew. Pearl was her best friend and married to Frank's older brother, Jason. They all lived on the Sterling family farm together, along with Frank and Jason's younger siblings. Quoting Alexandre Dumas, Pearl liked to say, "One for all and all for one," referring to the way the family members looked out for each other since Frank and Jason's parents died a little over a year ago.

The path meandered along the edge of the bluff overlooking the Minnesota River Valley where the oldest section of town lay. Mostly business buildings now lined the street below; most of the residences were built on the bluff. Windom Academy was off by itself on the edge of town. As they neared the houses, the smell of smoke from coal and wood fires drifted on the crisp air.

Frank stopped, looking out over the valley. "I love this view."

"I do, too," Amy agreed, "especially like this, when the lights shine through the evening snowfall."

Not many business lights were on at this time of night, but the street lamps were lit, and yellow squares shown from the saloon windows.

"Look." Frank pointed into the darkness. "People must be skating by the mill. See the bonfire beside the warming house?"

"I wish we'd thought to bring our blades." Sylvia's voice dripped disappointment.

"Let's arrange a skating party over the holidays," Amy suggested.

The others quickly agreed and decided the next night would be the perfect time.

The idea brought back to Amy memories of skating with Frank the previous winter at the Shakespearean Rink. She'd been surprised when he'd stopped beside her at the edge of the rink and asked her to skate. Many of the girls her age were hoping he'd show interest in them. He seldom did, not before and not after he asked to keep company with Amy.

She understood without Frank stating it that he was not a man who courted girls lightly. She'd wanted to honor his promise to prove his decision to give up drinking and gambling by not allowing other men to escort her during the past year.

"Foolish notion," her father had raved. "And what if young Sterling doesn't have the backbone to keep up the fight? You'll not waste your time waiting for him while other, more responsible men want to escort you."

"It isn't honorable to take the chance I might give my heart to another when I've promised him—"

"You've only promised to attend a church service with him, not to marry the man." Her father had stopped his tirade and looked over the top of his reading glasses to fix a better-tell-the-truth glare upon her. "At least you've told me of no other promise."

She'd felt her face heat. "I've made no other promise, but you made one. You promised him that if he didn't drink or gamble for a year, he could court me."

"Hmmmph. I didn't mean to imply formal courtship, only that I wouldn't object to him keeping company with you." Her father looked back at his paper. "Never told him you wouldn't be promised to someone else at the end of the year."

"I should think your promise implied I'd be free, and I intend to be free."

In the end, she'd reluctantly agreed to other escorts. She didn't tell her father she'd made a promise to herself not to allow any man to escort her more than once. "I won't tease them with the possibility of winning my affections," she'd vowed.

Joy filled her now, strolling with Frank in the midst of the warmth and laughter of friends. Still, she wished for private time together. She wanted to tell him how proud she was of him, that she knew his battle wasn't easy, that she'd prayed every day of the last year that God would give him strength. Would she have the courage to say these things if they were alone? Probably not, she admitted to herself. It would be too bold. He might think she was reminding him of their agreement to go to the service together.

The group dwindled as, one by one, they reached students' homes and said good night. There were only two girls and three young men left when they reached Amy's house. Laughing, they walked her up onto the broad porch and right to her door. "Wouldn't want you to slip again," Walter said, falling in beside her and Frank at the bottom of the steps and placing a hand under her elbow.

She stood inside the hall beside the open, etched-glass door and watched them leave, their voices and laughter fading. Did Frank glance back once over his shoulder at her, or did her wishful thinking make it appear so?

Amy closed the door slowly and rested her forehead against the glass. The heady joy of the evening began melting into doubt. Was it possible Frank had forgotten the promise to attend Christmas Eve services together?

two

Frank dismounted from his horse and tied the reins to the ring beside the horse stoop at the street in front of the Hendersons' home. He reached for the hat resting on the saddle horn, then turned and started up the walk toward the house.

"Hey, Frank, wait up."

Frank groaned. He forced a smile. "Hi." He'd forgotten Roland lived next door to Amy. He held the hat at his side, low, and slightly behind him, hoping his jacket would help conceal the dainty item.

Roland punched Frank's shoulder and winked. "I can guess what you're doing in this part of the woods. Heard you walked Miss Amy home last night."

"About a dozen of us, men and women, walked her home." Frank attempted to keep his tone emotionless.

"Hear tell it was your arm she was leanin' on."

"It was slippery out."

"Yes, it certainly was, especially in areas of the heart."

Frank gripped the hat brim tighter. *If he doesn't stop that irritating wink, I'll. . .* Frank couldn't think of anything his conscience would allow. He forced a lightness to his voice. "Think you're taking those romantic poets in English literature too seriously, Roland. You're seeing romance in everything."

Roland grinned. "Like in that fancy bonnet you're tryin' to hide?"

Frank's neck and face heated as though he stood too close to a woodstove. "Just returning the lady's hat. She lost it last night."

Roland's grin widened. "That must have been easy to do

on an innocent walk on a windless night in the middle of a crowd. I guess she forgot her hat pins at home."

"Excuse me." Frank brushed past Roland without looking at him. His indignation only earned him more laughter. When he reached the porch, he glanced over his shoulder. Roland's bouncy stride carried him away down the walk.

Anger dissipated when Amy opened the door. She looked a vision to him in her rose-colored dress with its high lace collar. Pleasant surprise shown in her eyes. "Hello, Frank. Won't you come in?"

He stepped inside the foyer and held out the tiny hat. "I came to return this."

She gasped and reached for it. "I can't believe you found it. I was certain it landed in some treetop, and come spring it would house a family of robins."

"Missed the treetops. I found it perched pretty as you please on a bush."

"I do hope you didn't spend hours and hours searching for it, though I am delighted to see it." Amy turned the hat about, examining it from every angle.

It had taken him the better part of the afternoon, and the bush was taller than his five feet seven inches, but he wasn't about to say so, or mention the snag the bush caused in his good trousers. "The hat doesn't look too much the worse for spending a night in the woods. That ribbon might need replacing, but the cloth flowers and the feathers are all right, I think. 'Course, me being a man, I don't rightly know for sure."

She fingered the maroon ribbon, her eyes sparkling in a smile. "Me being a woman," she mimicked, "I expect you're right."

He grinned, happy as a horse freed to pasture just to be looking at her and teasing with her.

"Oh, dear." Amy set the hat down on a marble-topped table beneath a gold-edged mirror. "Seeing my hat excited me so much that I forgot my manners. Won't you come in and visit?"

"I'd like to see your father, if he's in."

She hesitated only a moment, darting Frank a curious glance. "He's in the library. May I take your coat? Then I'll tell him you're here."

"I don't want to disturb him," Frank said, unbuttoning his jacket.

"I'm sure he'll be glad to speak with you." She hung his jacket and wide-brimmed hat on the mahogany hall tree's marble-tipped hooks before heading for the library.

Frank began pacing as soon as she left the hall. He stopped in front of the mirror and slicked back his hair. He wouldn't be more nervous if he were intending to ask permission to be Amy's only suitor. He'd like to ask that, but he knew the time wasn't right. He loved Amy and was reasonably sure she wasn't interested in anyone else. It was her father Frank believed wouldn't agree to a formal courtship yet.

Frank knew it was unusual for a young man to ask permission to court a girl in the everyday context of keeping company without the special privileges of a formal courtship. But Frank and Amy's situation was unusual. Frank had agreed to Mr. Henderson's demand to prove himself for a year. It was only fitting he ask the man's permission to keep company with Amy.

Frank shut his eyes and took a deep breath. "Please, Lord, let him say yes. And I could sure use some strength while meeting with him."

Amy returned and led him to the library. He ignored the curiosity in her eyes. He'd satisfy her questions when he knew the answers.

The room's somber elegance tested his already-strained courage. Bookcases on all but the outer wall reached to the ceiling, filled with books bound in blue, red, and brown leather with gold lettering. Mr. Henderson cast an imposing figure in the high-backed leather chair behind the mahogany desk, a shaft of late-afternoon sunlight from the tall window touching the white hair ringing his balding head. He wasn't wearing a suit jacket, but that was the only acquiescence he'd made to casual dress, Frank noted.

Mr. Henderson removed his reading glasses, rose, and extended his hand to Frank over the desktop. "Won't you be seated, Sterling? What can I do for you?"

Both men sat down, Frank in the leather wing chair facing the desk. His heart beat hard where his Adam's apple usually resided. "Sir, I'd like your permission to keep company with your daughter."

Henderson eyed him over pyramided fingertips. "I believe I set out my conditions to your intention last year."

"Yes, Sir."

"You were to stay sober and out of trouble for a year."

"Yes, Sir. I mean, I have, Sir."

"I hadn't forgotten the year was almost up. I spoke with Sheriff Amundson, asked him what he knows about your habits. He keeps a close eye on the saloons and billiard halls since so many fights break out at those establishments." The older man's eyes didn't blink or shift.

Frank tried to keep his gaze as steady as that he faced. He swallowed hard. Why be nervous? He hadn't anything to hide. "I haven't entered a saloon or billiard hall since before I gave my word to you and Amy, not even the temperance billiard hall."

"So Amundson said." Distrust filled the older man's voice.

Frank's heart sank. What could he say to prove his case if Mr. Henderson didn't believe the sheriff?

"A man can drink outside of a saloon," Henderson observed.

"I give you my word I haven't had a sip of liquor."

Henderson leaned his elbows on the desk. "You have my permission to ask Amy if she wishes to court you. I'll be honest with you. I prefer she court a man who never had a reason to reform. If I hear you've slipped back into your old ways, you will stop courting my daughter and never speak to her again."

"Yes, Sir. I won't slip." Frank stood and rubbed the palm of his hand quickly against his trouser leg before extending his hand. "Thank you, Sir."

Amy's father's lips tightened, but he shook hands. "Mind you, I'm not granting you the right to ask Amy to enter into a formal courtship. You may ask Amy to court you, but not exclusively."

"I understand, Sir."

The thick rug cushioned Frank's steps like the cloud he felt he walked on when he left the room. *Thank You, Lord. Thank You for giving me the backbone to ask him, and thank You that he said yes.*

He found Amy in the dining room arranging red carnations in a crystal bowl on the lace-covered dining-room table. "Business completed?" she asked with a small smile.

"Yes. At least, my business with your father. May I speak with you for a minute?"

"Of course." She stopped playing with the flowers and gave him her full attention.

He'd waited so long for this moment, and now he didn't know how to start. He shored up his courage with the reminder that less than twenty-four hours earlier she'd walked home from the Academy on his arm, apparently content to be close to him. "My business with your father involves you. You might recall the promise I made to him last year."

"Yes." A sweet flush brightened her cheeks.

"I kept that promise, Miss Amy, honest I did."

"I know that."

Her quiet assurance stopped his train of thought. "You do?"

"Of course. I knew you would keep it. You aren't a man who breaks his word."

Gratitude and wonder at her faith in him surged through him. Her lashes hid her eyes for a moment, then swept up in a shy manner. "Even so, I prayed for you."

"You did?"

She nodded. "Every night."

All those times he'd struggled to keep away from drink and gambling dens, thinking he was all alone in the fight, Amy's faith and the Lord had been alongside him. It humbled him. "You made a promise, too."

Her smile lit her eyes. "I thought you'd forgotten."

"Not likely." He grinned. "I've been living on that promise. That is. . .you don't need to keep it, you know." It was easier to say after seeing her smile.

"I don't go back on my word, either."

"I know." He paused, realizing his words echoed her faith in him. "I'm releasing you from your promise."

Her smile disappeared. "I see."

He could barely hear the words. *She thinks I don't want to go to the Christmas Eve service with her.* "I'm not saying this right." He ran a hand through his hair. "I only meant I don't want you to feel obligated to. . .to allow me to escort you. . . anywhere." He watched her serious gaze searching his. "I've waited a year to ask this, and now I've messed it up something fierce."

"What is your question?"

He took a deep breath and straightened his shoulders. "Miss Amy, would you do me the honor of attending the Christmas Eve service with me?"

"Yes."

He swiped his hands as if declaring a baseball runner safe. "Only if you want to, not because you feel obligated."

One side of her mouth tipped in a smile. "That's a bold question, Mr. Sterling, but I assure you I am not saying yes from a sense of obligation."

He grinned. "Good. I mean, I'm glad." He shifted his weight from one foot to the other and back again. "Guess I should be leaving."

"I'll see you to the door."

Coat, hat, and gloves back on, Frank stepped onto the porch. "Would you like to go skating? A bunch from the Academy are going to be at the Shakespearean Rink tonight."

"Thank you, but I can't. Father's invited a guest for dinner, and I'm expected to act as hostess."

Frank nodded, only slightly disappointed. The promise of Christmas Eve made it impossible to feel letdown. "I'll see you on Christmas Eve, then." He touched his hand to his hat brim and left.

Mounted on his horse, he glanced back at the house. He didn't see her watching from the door or window, but he waved just in case.

≈

Amy leaned back against the rose-embossed wallpaper beside the front door and sighed with pure joy. With eyes closed, she relived the last few minutes. "He didn't forget the promise after all," she whispered.

"Who are you talking to?" Her father's voice boomed out, startling her.

"Just me, myself, and I." She stood on tiptoe and kissed his cheek.

"I suppose that Sterling boy is the reason you're so bubbly."

"You know he is."

"It's unseemly to be so obvious about it. You're only courting, not engaged."

She laughed at his grumpy tone and slipped a hand under his arm. "You're just a poor loser. You didn't think he'd change."

"A leopard doesn't change its spots."

"Frank Sterling is a man, not a leopard. Men can change, especially when they let God help them."

"I'd rather you courted someone who didn't have any spots that needed changing, someone like Walter Bay."

Amy wrinkled her nose. "Oh, Father, please."

"Bay has a good business head on his shoulders. He's never been in trouble with the law, which is certainly more than you can say for Sterling. Walter Bay is good husband material."

"Now who is talking engagements? And to a man I haven't even courted."

"He's interested. I see it in his eyes when he's watching you. If he asks to court you, I want you to say yes."

"I don't care to court him."

"Bay hasn't the dark good looks that make Sterling so attractive to the girls in this town—"

"Frank doesn't act the Don Juan."

"Girls aren't the only ones who talk. Parents do, too. I know girls like his looks. Bay probably seems plain and staid to you beside Sterling, but he's settled and steady, and that's a good thing for a woman."

A slight shudder ran through her. "There's something about him I can't place my finger on, but it makes me distrust him. Besides, what about Frank? You've already given your blessing to our courting."

"Permission, not blessing." He laid his hands on her shoulders. "Choosing a husband is serious business. A girl's heart isn't always the best judge of what's good for her." He sighed deeply. "I wish your mother were here to advise you about men."

And everything else, she thought. The five years since her mother's death had been hard on both her and her father. She crossed her arms and gave her father a teasing glance. "Mother would be supporting me and giving advice to you about the men in my life."

Her quip brought a chuckle, but he didn't change his tune. "You haven't let any of the many men interested in you buzz around for long. I think you're only interested in Sterling because I placed a 'no trespassing' sign in front of him for the last year."

"Father!"

"I told him he could ask you to court him, but not ask you to court him exclusively."

"I won't be one of those girls who teases men, trying to make them jealous and keep them guessing as to my affections. It's disrespectful. You know you wouldn't like it if I acted that way."

"All I'm asking is that you don't settle for less of a man than you deserve."

"I won't, Father."

He chucked her under the chin she'd raised in defiance. "Give Walter a chance. Be nice to him at dinner tonight."

three

Amy was polite to Walter during the meal, but her mind drifted to Frank and the service they'd attend together in a few days. Conversation flowed easily between Walter and her father. Their common views on business and finance were apparent as they discussed the silver question, the labor element warring against capitalists, and the unemployment and poor economic conditions following the Panic of '93.

The two men had met in the library for almost an hour before dinner. She hoped that meant they'd resolved any personal business and Walter wouldn't be staying long into the evening. She sighed behind her napkin when her father instructed the maid to serve after-dinner coffee in the parlor.

Amy's years of training in deportment and duty came to her assistance as always. She smiled pleasantly while pouring coffee for the men from the silver teapot and asking Walter's preference in cream and sugar.

Walter's gaze bore into hers as she handed him the china cup. She resented his rudeness and turned her attention to serving her father.

"You have a beautiful home, Mr. Henderson."

"Thank you, but that compliment belongs to my wife. It was her gift for making a building into a home that gave beauty to this house. She and I lived in a number of homes over the years, but no others were as special as this one."

"Not many homes in this part of the country compare to it, Sir."

"It's not the grandeur that gives it worth." Mr. Henderson's voice held a hint of reproof. "It's precious because my wife loved it and because it's the last place where we were together. Amy is the only thing I treasure more than this home."

Amy felt a painful lump form in her throat. Her father had loved her mother deeply. Did life sometimes seem unbearable to him without her?

After a moment Walter cleared his throat. Amy wondered whether her father's revealing personal comments had made their guest uncomfortable.

"Are you planning to join our friends at the ice rink tonight, Miss Amy?" Walter asked. "A number of the local Windom students are gathering there this evening," he explained to Mr. Henderson.

"Amy hasn't mentioned it. I hope you two don't think you need to entertain me." He waved a hand in a dismissing motion. "Go, enjoy yourselves. If I were young and spry, I'd head down there myself."

"That's kind of you, Sir. If Miss Amy would—"

"I enjoy spending my evenings with you, Father." Amy hoped her consternation didn't show in her quick reply.

"Spoken like a dutiful daughter, but I'm sure you'd prefer spending time with your friends. Run upstairs and change clothes."

Fury set Amy's hands to trembling so that she barely kept her cup and saucer from rattling. "I wouldn't want to impose myself upon Mr. Bay, Father."

"It's no imposition, I assure you." Walter's eyes sparkled in what to Amy seemed wicked glee.

Twenty minutes later she came down dressed in her emerald green skating outfit.

"Didn't you have a new skating outfit made?" her father asked.

"I'm keeping it for the new year." She hoped to wear the new outfit with Frank. Her pleasure in it would be removed if she wore it with Walter.

She hugged her father good-bye at the door. "You practically demanded I go with Walter tonight. How could you?" she whispered in his ear. "This is a low, mean trick."

He patted her back, and his voice held laughter. "Yes, yes, I hope you have a wonderful time." He beamed while waving them out the door.

The walk to the rink through the crisp early evening air did nothing to cool Amy's temper. Even the sounds of blades against ice and voices raised in fun didn't calm the fire in her chest. She answered questions posed by Walter politely but introduced no topics of conversation herself. A sliver of guilt stabbed at her. Was her attitude unfair toward Walter? After all, her father was the one who'd pushed them together. It only appeared that the two men had conspired together against her. Or did it?

The rink brought back memories of skating with Frank the previous year. They'd only skated together a few minutes, but those minutes comprised one of her favorite times. She'd loved the way his arm held her gently yet firmly snug against his side. She'd loved his gentle but shy gaze when he'd looked into her eyes. They'd skated in lovely unison, and for those few minutes no one else had existed in her world.

And to think she'd turned down Frank's invitation to skate tonight only to be forced to come with Walter.

In the middle of the rink, a bunch of boys were playing crack the whip, their screams filled half with fear and half with fun. Older boys flirted by, dashing in and out between girls who skated sedately along the rink's edge. Couples skated arm-in-arm, the women's skirts swaying.

Amy's gaze searched the rink for friends. Figures moved in and out of the shadows and light cast by the rinkside lanterns. "There's Roland." She pointed him out to Walter, laughing. Seeing other friends lifted her spirits. "He's up to his usual pranks, skating circles around Sylvia and her sister."

"Maybe he'll keep them so busy they won't see us. Sylvia could talk the ear off a stalk of corn."

"I like her friendly manner. She never speaks unkindly of people." *Unlike present company.*

A couple whirled up to the rink's edge with a flashy turn. "Hello, Amy."

"Pearl, Jason, hello," she greeted Frank's brother and sister-in-law. Their cheeks were cherry red and their eyes bright with fun. "How nice you could make it in from the farm."

Jason pulled his wife close with one arm. "Couldn't miss a perfect skating night like this."

Walter took Amy's elbow. "Let's get our skating boots on and join them out on the ice."

Amy saw the surprise and question in Pearl's eyes at Walter's proprietary touch. Slipping her skating boots from where they'd hung on her shoulder effectively removed his hand for the moment.

Friends of all ages called and waved to them as they made their way toward the bonfire in front of the warming house. The wood smoke seemed to warm Amy's lungs before she and Walter reached the group standing about the crackling fire. She sat down on a log that was already brushed free of snow and began to unbutton a boot.

"Let me help you with that." Walter knelt in the snow in front of her.

Annoyance flickered across her chest when his hands brushed her fingers away from her boot. "Please, Walter, I—"

"Amy."

Her head shot up at the strangled sound of her name. Behind Walter stood Frank, disbelief and betrayal in his eyes.

❧

Frank didn't wait for a response. The surprise in Amy's eyes showed she hadn't expected to see him. Frank turned on his heel and headed toward the street and his horse. Pain cinched his chest like a tight saddle belt. He brushed past people, not caring whether he knew them.

He climbed into the saddle and turned his horse toward home. The sound of piano music and laughter from Plummer's Saloon down the street caught his attention. He hesitated, remembering the way amber-colored beer slid down the throat so easily, the way problems slid away after a few drinks, and the pleasant camaraderie of others who cooled burning hearts with liquor. A way to ease the pain was so close, only a short way down the main street.

He pressed his lips together tight and nudged his horse with his knees. "Let's get home, Boy."

His pain didn't ease as he rode out of town, down the straight, empty, rutted road toward the farm. The cold air didn't ease the burning in his stomach caused by the memory of Walter Bay's hand on Amy's boot. How could she allow such intimate contact only hours after agreeing to permit him, Frank, to court her?

He'd thought she wanted that as much as he did. The way her eyes lit up when he asked her to the Christmas Eve service, her assurance that she'd been praying for him, her insistence that she was agreeing to see him because she wanted to, not because she felt obligated, all led him to believe she cared.

"I'm a fool. A certified, one hundred percent fool."

He hadn't asked her to court him exclusively, or at all, he realized. He'd only asked her to attend the Christmas Eve service with him. He'd assumed she wouldn't be any more interested in courting others than he was. Evidently he'd assumed wrong.

But the worst, what cut straight into his heart, was the lie. "She didn't say she was going skating with someone else. She said she was hostessing a dinner for her father."

His horse tossed its head as though trying to look back at

him and snorted. Frank patted its neck. "I'm not talking to you, Boy."

Frank had never been interested in any girl but Amy. Even when they were children, he'd liked her quiet ways. She'd always befriended the shy students at school.

She'd won his heart when they were ten. The class had spent a fun morning capturing butterflies. The next morning the class arrived at school to find all the butterflies gone. When the angry teacher demanded who had released them, Amy quietly admitted her act. He liked that she wanted the butterflies to be free, that she'd had the courage to set them free and the courage to admit she was the guilty party.

He'd watched her grow into a serene, strong, beautiful young woman. The more he learned about her, the more he admired her. That made the thought she'd lied to him all the more painful.

This afternoon his world had looked brighter than a snow-covered field in sunshine. Now even the light looked dark.

❧

Amy's heart tossed and upended like a tumbleweed rolling across the prairie. The pain in Frank's eyes insisted on interfering with her vision and played havoc with her usual smooth skating strokes. She tripped herself and Walter repeatedly. After causing a tangled heap of fellow skaters for the fifth time, she held up her mittened hands in resignation. "I'm sorry. It's my first time on skates this year."

Walter helped her to her feet and slid an arm around her waist. "My arm's available to lean on."

Amy shifted away. "I need to practice staying upright under my own power." She hoped her excuse softened the sting of her repeated moves away from him. She preferred more forthright behavior, but her father's desire that she spend time with Walter kept a guard on her tongue. The only familiarity she allowed Walter was to hold her hand over a rough patch of ice.

She excused herself twice to skate with Pearl. Walter skated uninvited beside them. His presence prevented Amy from sharing with Pearl her frustration over Walter's escort. If only she could manage a few minutes alone with her friend, she knew Pearl would relate the truth of the situation to Frank.

Amy watched in dismay as Pearl and Jason left before Amy found the private moment she'd hoped for. She had no desire to stay after Pearl left.

"It's a perfect skating night, but I'm cold, Walter."

"Some time by the fire will warm you up. There's popcorn to warm your insides, too."

"I'd rather go home."

"It's early yet."

"Maybe it's all the falls I've taken tonight that have tired me." It was worrying over Frank's reaction to seeing her with Walter that had tired her, but her mother's social training was hard to overcome. "Please don't feel you need to escort me home. I'll understand if you prefer to stay here with your friends."

His eyes glittered in the light of the lantern at rinkside. "There's no one here whose company I prefer to yours. Let me help you with your skates."

The wooden stairs leading up the ridge from Main Street to the residential streets on the prairie above were slippery with frost. Walter insisted on keeping one hand on her back "for safety" even though she kept one hand on the wooden banister. Amy reflected with an aching heart how coldly she responded to his touch and assistance compared to her reaction to Frank's care for her the previous night.

They were both breathing a bit harder when they reached the top of the steps across the street from the new, three-story brick school. They turned left and started toward her home.

"I was impressed with your sketching ability last night," Walter complimented. "Professor Headley tells me you'll be teaching an art course at the Academy next quarter."

At last a subject she could discuss with pleasure. "Yes. I'm flattered he asked me to teach. In spite of the wonderful reception my work received at the Minnesota Exhibition in St. Paul last year, I know I have much to learn."

"You're being modest."

"Not at all. I'd love to study the masters."

"What's preventing you?"

"I'd need to travel to Europe."

He stopped, a stunned look on his face. "You speak as if you were planning to become an artist."

She lifted her chin to look him squarely in the eye. "I am an artist."

"I know, but it's only a hobby, isn't it? Certainly no woman with a true feminine soul would travel about the world unchaperoned simply to study art. Besides, from what I understand, some pictures are hardly suitable for a woman to view."

Amy began walking, her stride lengthening. How dare he comment on her character and artistic ambitions? He hadn't even waited to hear what she wanted to do with her painting before condemning her interest in it. Blood pounded in her ears, warning her to calm down before speaking.

"Careful." Walter caught her elbow. "You've fallen enough on the ice tonight. You don't want to fall here, too."

She thought she needed more care with her tongue than her feet. Perhaps the way to avoid more attacks on herself was to direct attention toward him. "What are your ambitions, Mr. Bay?"

Usually she considered the social requirement of calling young men she'd known since knee-pants days by their surname silly, though she normally complied with it. But on this occasion, the rule provided a convenient way to gently inform

Walter that she wasn't interested in moving beyond friendship. Hopefully he would take the hint.

"My business is doing well in Chippewa City for the moment. I plan to eventually expand my real-estate and loan business across a broader area, perhaps relocate to a larger city."

"I'm sure you'd do well in a larger town." Everyone knew everyone else in Chippewa City. Walter might be able to draw the wool over the eyes of the older businessmen such as her father, but those closer to his own age weren't fooled by his false charm. In a city where people didn't know him so well, she thought, he might do better; although she had to admit he was doing quite well already. "Father has mentioned your fine business mind more than once."

"Ah, I'm glad to hear someone is praising my virtues to you."

This wasn't the direction she wanted the conversation to go.

They turned into the walk to her house. "I'd like to escort you to the Christmas Eve service, Miss Amy."

Surprise left her speechless. For a year she'd thought of attending the service with Frank. It never occurred to her that someone else might ask to accompany her.

At the bottom of the front steps, Walter stopped her with his hand on her arm. "Did you hear me?"

"Yes." At least he'd waited until now to ask. The painted parlor lamp in the window shed comforting light over the porch and onto her and Walter. "Your invitation surprises me. I—"

"I'm sure you've noticed my interest in you lately." Amusement tinged his voice.

Amy nodded. "Yes." She took a deep breath. "Thank you for honoring me with your invitation, Mr. Bay, but I've already agreed to join Mr. Sterling at the Christmas Eve service."

"Ah." He clasped his hands behind his back and lowered his gaze to the walk. "I'm sure you are too much the lady to rescind your acceptance of Sterling's invitation?" He glanced up beneath raised eyebrows.

She almost laughed at his conceit, for his inflection indicated he hoped she would change her mind. "Yes, I am, Mr. Bay." Amy stilled her smile. She wanted to honor her father, but she simply could not continue seeing this man. She adjusted her already straight shoulders, giving herself courage. "I must tell you that I never allow anyone to escort me more than once. I realize your invitation is a great compliment, and it is with respect for that honor that I ask you not to ask me again."

His expression didn't change. His gaze seemed to study hers, though Amy couldn't be certain in the lamplight. "Not ask you again to attend the Christmas Eve service, or not ask to escort you again to anything?"

Her fingers gripped the laces of her skates tighter, but she kept her gaze and voice steady. "Anything."

Walter burst into laughter.

Amy stared at him. No men had responded to her refusals with mirth before.

He stepped toe-to-toe with her. She wanted to step back, but she was at the edge of the walk and didn't care to step into the snow.

Walter took her chin between his thumb and index finger and jerked her chin up.

Shock rippled through her.

He brought his face close to hers. His eyes appeared black with anger. She tried to pull her head back, but he tightened his hold on her chin. "Your innocence is endearing, but make no mistake, I will escort you again, and you will welcome my escort."

He released her so suddenly she almost stumbled.

Walter stepped back. "In fact, my dear Miss Henderson, not only will we court, but we will marry."

Amy's mouth dropped open.

Walter bowed deeply. Then, with a laugh, he left.

four

Fury still roiled in place of Amy's usual calm the next morning. She donned an apron and joined Lina, the maid who had been with the family for ten years, cleaning the downstairs in an attempt to work off her anger. Amy's thoughts continued to center on Walter's uncouth behavior rather than on housely duties.

"Watch out!" Lina caught a china figurine before it hit the pale blue etched parlor rug. "Miss Amy, you yield that feather duster like a weapon."

"I've something prickly on my mind." She brushed back a lock of hair that had fallen from its upsweep. "Thank you for catching the figurine. Mother loved that lady. I would never have forgiven myself if I'd broken it."

"You are a pure danger in here." Lina gently took the duster from Amy's hand. "Why don't you put on a pretty outfit and get out of the house? Surely there must be something you still need to buy for Christmas."

"Perhaps that's a good idea." Amy untied her apron strings while she headed to her room to change into her tailored tweed gown. Knocking the figurine from its place on the mahogany wall shelf had jolted the fury out of her and left her with a bone-melting weariness.

Walking down to the shops in the crisp morning sunshine rejuvenated her body and spirits. School was out, and children were everywhere: playing fox and geese, building snowmen, launching snowballs from behind white fort walls, flailing their arms as they made snow angels, and filling the air with their whoops above flying sleds and shovels.

Amy's hatbox swung from her arm by its gold satin string. The pretty little hat in need of a new ribbon rested inside. By the time she reached Miss Hermanson's Millinery, she'd regained her usual serenity.

Miss Hermanson's hands fluttered about the hat. "Mm, mm, mmm. Poor thing. It's been through a bout, hasn't it? Well, never mind. I'll replace the ribbon, and it will be good as new. Of course, it will take a bit of doing, as the ribbon winds in and out over the standing feathers and flowers. The matching bow in front will need to be replaced, too."

"I know you're awfully busy with the holidays upon us, but could you possibly have it ready by Christmas Eve?" Amy gave her most apologetic smile.

The millinery artist hesitated only a moment. "For you, of course."

"Thank you. I can't tell you how much it means to me." Amy's gloved hand gave Miss Hermanson's fingers a quick squeeze. The tinkling bells above the door reflected Amy's lighter heart as she left the store.

She stopped in front of the window at Sherdahl Jewelers, her attention caught by a large snow globe. In it a couple skated, joined forever above the walnut music-box base. The image brought back the sweet joy of skating with Frank. That pleasure was immediately shadowed by the memory of his eyes when he saw her the previous night with Walter, and her heart crimped.

Amy turned abruptly, blinking back tears. *I don't remember when I've been such an emotional puddle.*

She hurried into the general store next door and turned to a display counter away from other customers and clerks, hoping to hide her telltale face. The move only brought her to a collection of mustache cups, which reminded her of Frank. She laughed at a caricature of a man with a narrow mustache with elaborately curled ends, which decorated one mug. If she and Frank had been courting for awhile, she would purchase it for him, just for fun.

No telling if he'd court her after last night. What if he didn't come to take her to the Christmas Eve service? The thought brought her up short. A moment later she shook her head. Frank Sterling was too much the gentleman to go back on his word that way. She turned from the display with a sigh.

That's quite enough of your self-pity. Think about someone else. Young people could always be found at Arnold's Ice Cream Parlor. It was just the place to get her mind off Frank.

Half a dozen Academy students were gathered about one of the tables in the parlor. Their warm welcome cheered her and convinced her she'd chosen the right place. The group was all a-chatter with holiday plans: house parties, dances, sledding, and sleighing.

Amy's enjoyment dimmed when Walter joined the group. The others' greetings to him weren't as friendly as they'd been for her, but they invited him to join in their parties. He smiled and laughed with everyone, but Amy had a hard time avoiding his gaze, which seemed pinned on her most of the time. She told herself she only thought it was so because of their altercation the night before; yet whenever she glanced in his direction, his gaze met hers with that laughing warning she'd seen in it in the dim lamplight.

When the group left, Amy purposely walked between Sylvia and her sister. Walter circumvented her attempt to avoid him by catching her elbow from behind and asking in a loud, overly friendly voice, "May I speak with you a moment, Miss Henderson? I'd like to ask your opinion on a gift for my mother."

Reluctance crawled through her, but she allowed herself to be drawn to his side in order to avoid drawing undue attention from the group. "I can't give an opinion on a gift. I don't know your mother, Mr. Bay, remember?"

"But you have excellent taste. I'm trying to choose between

two perfumes. Will you stop at Heiberg and Torgerson's with me and see which scent you prefer?"

"One's preference in scent is so personal. I'm not sure—"

"Please."

She nodded curtly, wishing she hadn't been raised "to be a lady," as her mother would state it.

They said their good-byes to the others and turned toward Heiberg and Torgerson's. As soon as they were out of her friends' hearing, Amy stopped. She gently pulled her arm away from Walter and clutched her black reticule at her waist with both hands. "Mr. Bay, I had no wish to embarrass either of us before our friends, but I have no intention of assisting you in something as personal as selecting a gift for your mother. I thought I made my feelings clear last night—"

"You made them most clear. I thought I made my intentions clear, too."

Heat flooded her cheeks in spite of the cold. "I'm sure your words were spoken in jest."

"Think again. I've something you should see." He undid the top buttons of his coat, pulled an envelope from an inner pocket, and held it out toward her.

Dread coiled within her. She took a step back, coming up against the general-store window. She didn't know why she reacted so strongly to his gesture, but she knew with absolute certainty she didn't want to touch that envelope. "What is it?"

"The mortgage papers on your home."

Her gaze shot from the envelope to his face. "That's ridiculous. Why should you have them?"

"A lot of banks have gone under in these hard times. I've bought up a number of loans, including your father's."

Her hold on her reticule tightened. "Why are you telling me this?"

"Your father, like so many men, is behind in his payments."

"You're lying. Father is extremely wise in financial matters.

He'd never allow his payments to lapse, nor would he dishonor a debt."

"You're right about his intentions. He assures me he intends to pay every penny he owes."

She adjusted her shoulders. This conversation was getting tiresome. "Then I repeat, why are you telling me this?"

Walter moved casually to her side and leaned against the building. "I intend to call his loan."

It took a moment for her mind to grasp the words. "You're going to require him to pay it off completely?"

He nodded, his eyes watching her face.

"But surely the contract requires the payments to be spread over a number of years." She'd learned a few things from growing up with a father who loved business.

"The contract states the loan can be called if he gets behind in payments. He's behind, way behind."

Her heart skipped a beat. She held out her hand. "I'd like to see the papers, please." She removed the papers from the envelope and scanned the agreement. There were the awful words in black and white with her father's signature at the bottom. Walter wasn't lying. He could demand payment. Slowly she refolded the papers, returned them to the envelope, and handed them back.

"He can't pay it, you know." Walter's tone was almost gentle.

Amy couldn't understand why she didn't feel anything. She'd been furious last night and this morning at Walter's presumption that she'd marry him, yet now his challenge to her father left her numb. "Why are you doing this?"

"Do you know the best thing about money?"

She waited, watching him.

"Power. You can make people do almost anything if you have money and they don't."

Disgust made her nauseous. "What is it you want?"

"You, Amy. I want you for my wife."

five

Amy's stomach turned over. She couldn't pull her gaze from Walter's laughing one. "You can't be serious."

"I assure you I am most serious. I will call your father's loan if you don't agree to marry me. It will bankrupt him."

She stared at him, unable to speak. *This is a nightmare. In a few minutes I'll awaken, and Father and I will have a hearty laugh over it.*

Walter touched a gloved finger to the brim of his brown derby. "I'll let you think on it until tomorrow. Why don't I take you to dinner? You can give me your answer then."

She watched him walk away, helplessness swirling through her like snow in a blizzard. Slowly anger rose up. He was lying, of course, trying to manipulate her. How could he think she would believe him? Her father was a wealthy man. Did Walter truly believe she would so easily fall into his trap?

Perhaps he only wanted her to agree to his terms so he could laugh at her. Maybe it was all a trick to repay her for telling him she didn't wish to court him.

But the mortgage papers were real.

She started toward home. Her thoughts raced faster than the heels of her boots clicking against the boardwalk. Just because the papers were real didn't mean it was true that her father was behind in payments or that he wasn't able to pay off the loan if it was called. He had lots of investments. Surely, if necessary, he could liquidate them.

What was happening to her life? She'd always considered herself a peace-filled person. The last two days she'd hardly known a peaceful moment, and all the disturbance was due to Walter Bay.

Her heart turned to the One she'd always trusted. *Dear Lord, please help Father and me, and keep us in the peace of Christ.*

Immediately Romans 8:35 flashed into her mind. "Who shall separate us from the love of Christ?"

"No one, Lord," she whispered into the winter wind that tugged at her scarf, "not even Walter Bay."

❧

Amy reminded herself of that verse more than once as the day and evening progressed. Peace was illusive, slipping in and out of her heart. "How shall I approach Father about his finances, Lord?" she asked. She was sure the Lord answered her, but she couldn't hear the answer; her mind whirled with questions and fears that made her deaf to the Lord's voice.

At dinner with her father that night, she watched the candlelight play off the crystal while she continued to study the problem. When she'd asked her father last summer if she might buy the new crystal pattern, he'd immediately said yes, as he did to all her requests. She couldn't recall a single instance in which he'd asked her to economize.

Mrs. Jorgenson stepped into the room, and Amy's gaze swerved to her. The cook surveyed the table to see whether any items needed replenishing.

"We're fine for now, Mrs. J." Father beamed at her. "This roast is done to perfection."

Mrs. Jorgenson's smile filled her broad Scandinavian face as she retreated into the kitchen.

Would Father keep Mrs. Jorgenson's and Lina's services if he were bankrupt? Amy wondered.

"Amy."

"Yes, Father?"

His eyes beneath heavy white eyebrows twinkled with amusement. "I've asked twice how you spent your day."

"I'm sorry. I guess I was woolgathering." She told him of her trip to the millinery and meeting her friends at the ice-cream parlor and the many plans for holiday parties, but left out Mr. Bay and his revelations.

"Are you attending any parties tonight?" he asked.

"No. Most of the evening parties are planned for between Christmas and New Year's. There's a tobogganing party tomorrow afternoon, but Lina and I will be baking for Christmas."

"Don't forget you begin teaching at the Academy when classes resume. You need to take time during the school break for fun."

"Preparing for Christmas is fun."

He chuckled. "You sound like your mother. Remember how she baked for days and days before Christmas and gave most of it away?"

"Yes." She smiled at their shared remembrance. "Mother loved decorating the house for Christmas, too. She always sang while she put up the greens and arranged flowers."

Her father's gaze moved slowly around the dining room. "She only had one Christmas here. We spent years planning the house before we built it."

Amy's heart caught at the tears that glistened in his eyes. It would break his heart to lose this house that he'd been so proud to give her mother. She looked down at her plate and pushed idly with her fork at a piece of roast beef. "Father, I've been wondering. . . ." Her voice trailed off. It seemed so rude to ask him about his money.

"What have you been wondering?"

"There are so many people with money problems because of the Panic. Are you. . .are things. . ."

He snorted. "Does it look like we're living at the poor farm? Don't you worry your head about money. I've always taken care of you, haven't I?"

"Yes, but—"

"And I always will." He winked. "At least until some young man takes over that responsibility."

Her smile felt feeble. His answer didn't reassure her at all.

❧

The next afternoon Amy saw her opportunity when her father left the house "to pick up one last thing for Christmas," as he said.

"Thank You, Lord," she said aloud, entering the library. The words were barely past her lips when she groaned. Was it wrong to thank God for a chance to go through her father's papers without his knowledge or permission?

Standing with her back to the window, she faced the desk. Where to begin? She started in the most obvious place, the drawer in the middle. Why should he be secretive? He wouldn't think he had anything to hide from anyone in his own home. She sat down in her father's leather chair and looked into the drawer.

"Go away," she murmured under her breath at the guilt that tugged at her conscience.

It didn't take long to go through all the drawers. Nothing she found yielded answers to her questions. She leaned back in the chair, gripping the arms. The next place to look was the safe, of course. Her father had told her the combination months ago. "In case anything should happen to me and you need to get into it," he'd said.

She knew Walter Bay's ultimatum wasn't what he'd meant. She crossed the room and removed a set of Shakespeare's works from a bookshelf to reveal the safe. "Forgive me," she murmured, reaching for the combination dial.

It was all there: ledgers, bankbooks, stock certificates, notes for loans. She carried the stack to the desk. Trepidation tightened her chest as she opened the ledger.

It didn't take long to discover Walter was correct. Her father had lost money on his investments when the market collapsed over a year ago. She saw that he'd lent money to others during those hard times, though he'd never spoken of it. Pride in him warmed her chest. It was like him to honor others' privacy. The ledger showed most of those people hadn't made payments in months. Knowing her father, she doubted he'd pressed for payments. He'd trust the people to pay when they were able again.

The original mortgage on the house had almost been paid off when the Panic hit. He'd taken out another mortgage to cover the income he'd lost. Like so many others during these hard times, he'd purchased food and other necessities on credit. Aside from the horses, Amy found no indication of assets other than the house and its contents that could provide the money to pay off Walter.

Her teaching wouldn't pay much, not enough to cover one monthly payment. Her paintings were beginning to sell, but she hadn't sold enough to make a dent in her father's debt. She dropped her head into her hands and groaned.

What money I did make on my paintings went back into painting supplies. Why didn't Father tell me we were having money problems? Does Father know of Walter's offer to forestall foreclosure if I marry him? Is that why Father pressed Walter's virtues as a husband yesterday? She shook her head vigorously. *No, Father would never concede to such a demand. Father would have thrown Walter out of the house if he'd suggested such a thing.*

The picture brought immense pleasure. It lasted only a moment. It was within her power to save her father's reputation and the home he treasured. How could she consider saving herself at his expense?

"Lord, I beg You, show me a way to save us both."

If only there were someone she could go to with her dilemma. If only she could share it with Frank. There was no one she would trust more. But he was the last person she could tell about Walter's awful demand.

❧

When Walter arrived at the front door that evening, Amy slipped into her black wool jacket and stepped onto the porch. The smile he gave her turned her stomach.

"Good evening." He offered her his arm. "I thought we'd go to the hotel for dinner, if that suits you."

"I am not going to dinner with you."

His face hardened. "We agreed to discuss the, uh, matter over dinner."

"You decided we would do so." Amy clutched her arms over her unbuttoned coat against the winter chill. "I will not go to dinner with a blackmailer."

"Blackmailer? I prefer to call myself an astute businessman."

Amy glared at him. She saw no point in arguing with him over trifles.

He spread his arms. "Have you asked your father if what I said is true?"

"I didn't tell him of your. . .offer."

A smile formed slowly. "I didn't think you would."

"It appears you are correct concerning Father's finances." Her stomach tightened with the admission. It seemed a betrayal to her father to admit the truth to this loathsome man.

The smile grew. "Then you have an answer to my proposal?"

"Proposal? I believe you mean bribery."

"Your answer?"

Amy tapped one toe against the floor planks. "What assurance do I have that if I agree to. . .to m. . .marry you that you will keep your agreement and not call my father's loan?"

He removed his brown derby and held it over his heart in an exaggerated gesture. "You have my word."

"Mr. Bay, your word would not purchase you a cup of coffee."

His chuckle would have infuriated her if she were not already angrier than ever before. Most men she knew would take offense to the implication their word meant nothing. Walter's amusement showed her he believed she had no choice but to marry him.

"What proof do you demand, Miss Amy?"

"Your signature on the mortgage papers, saying the loan is paid in full."

His voice hardened. "That's not the deal I'm offering. If you marry me, I won't call the loan immediately. I'll allow your father to pay when he is able. That's the deal."

"I'm not so foolish as to trust you to keep that promise. In return for me, I want your signature agreeing that Father's mortgage is completely paid, including interest on past due payments. That's this year's price for a purchased bride."

"You aren't in a position to bargain."

"No?" Amy raised her eyebrows and gave him her sweetest smile. "How many men in this town will continue to do business with you once they hear you tried to buy a wife by threatening to drive her father into bankruptcy?"

Walter studied her gaze, bouncing his derby against one thigh.

She met his gaze without blinking, continuing to smile. It wouldn't do for him to know she was quaking inside. Would he guess she'd never expose her father's situation to the town in such a sordid manner, that her challenge was pure effrontery?

"You wouldn't do that, Amy. I heard your father say the only thing he loves more than this house is you. You're too much the loving, devoted daughter to allow him to lose his house and his reputation to boot."

The sliver of hope she'd held to dissolved. He was right, of course.

"Your revelations might hurt my business," Walter conceded, "but at a steep cost to your father. I admit, though, your idea has some merit. You're an only child, and your father is a widow. Upon his death, all he has will belong to us. Requiring him to pay off the loan is only taking money from myself. I won't receive it as soon this way, but I'll receive it just the same."

Horror left her speechless.

"I'll sign over the mortgage right after the ceremony," Walter conceded.

Amy shook her head slowly. "Before the ceremony."

"Oh, no." He shook a finger at her. "How do I know you'll go through with the ceremony if I give the executed note to you first?"

"How do I know you will keep your promise if the note isn't signed before the ceremony?"

"It seems we're at an impasse." He grinned. "Or we would be at an impasse if you had anything with which to bargain."

What a couple we'll make, neither of us trusting the other. She shoved away the despair the thought brought to her. "Sign the note in my presence before the ceremony. We'll give it to the pastor. After the ceremony, the pastor can return it to us, and you can present it to Father."

Amy held her breath, waiting for Walter's answer. He was maddeningly slow in giving it.

"Agreed. Not much chance you'll back out in front of the preacher, not right before the ceremony."

The small triumph didn't bring her joy. "You can tell Father you wouldn't think of holding him to his debt since you're family." Amy couldn't keep the sarcasm from her voice.

"A wedding gift. I like the idea. Not many grooms make their fathers-in-law such generous gifts." His smile held self-satisfaction. "A few well-placed references, and word will spread around town. It should be great for business."

Hopelessness swirled through Amy's chest. Walter managed to turn every attempt she made to insure her father's home and reputation into another victory for himself.

Walter leaned toward her. "One more thing. I want our engagement announced at the Christmas Eve service."

six

"No!" The word burst from Amy. She struggled for composure. She simply couldn't give up the evening with Frank. "It wouldn't be proper to announce it then."

"I won't allow this to drag out."

"I've already committed to attending the Christmas Eve service with Frank Sterling."

Walter snorted. "Uncommit yourself."

"If I'm willing to break my word to him, why would you trust my promise to marry you?"

"I doubt Sterling offers the same incentive I do."

"He doesn't need to use chicanery. He's a gentleman."

"He isn't the man you've promised to marry. I'd rather be your groom than a gentleman."

"I won't agree to formalizing the engagement until after Christmas Eve."

"Immediately after."

She hesitated. She didn't want to become engaged any sooner than necessary but couldn't think of any way to extend her freedom. "All right."

"Christmas Day." Walter stepped closer. "How about a kiss for your future groom?"

"Not until you are my groom in fact."

"You are one challenging woman, Amy Henderson." Walter grinned and donned his brown derby. "I admire the fight in you. I'd no idea you had the stomach for bargaining. You might actually be good at it one day with me around for an example. Just one word of warning." His gaze hardened. "Don't ever try bargaining against me again."

He turned around at the top of the porch steps. "You and I are going to make a great team, after I train you in a bit."

A dubious compliment at best, Amy thought.

At least she wouldn't be spending Christmas Eve with him. It seemed incongruous to think of attending the service in his company. He was faithful in attending church, but if he loved God, his actions certainly didn't reveal it. She suspected his church involvement was all show, considered necessary for his image as an upstanding citizen.

She groaned as a new realization struck. On top of everything else, had she agreed to marry a man who didn't share her faith? She knew the Bible admonished against Christians marrying non-Christians. It wasn't one of the commandments, but that didn't mean she could take the admonition casually.

If she and Walter didn't share a faith in the Lord, how could it be God's will that they marry? Yet how else could her father keep the house?

"I asked You to show me a way to save myself and Father from Walter's intentions, Lord. If You've shown me that way, I haven't recognized it yet. Open my eyes to Your way and my ears to Your voice, Lord," she whispered, shivering as she watched Walter disappear into the dusk.

&

Frank stepped out of the sleigh he'd rented at the livery and tied the dapple gray to the hitching-post ring in front of Amy's home. Light from the lantern at the front of the sleigh made moving shadows across the snow as the horse shifted.

Frank nodded a bit self-consciously at a young family walking past dressed in Sunday best. "Merry Christmas." *On their way to church*, he thought. Where he and Amy would be headed in a few minutes. This last week's confusion had dimmed the anticipation of the evening he'd looked forward to for so long. *Why did Amy lie to me about going skating with*

Walter Bay? The question had haunted him. What if when he showed up at her house to take her to church she had changed her mind?

She wouldn't do that. She was not that kind of girl.

He hadn't thought she was the kind of girl to lie, either.

Frank's feet had brought him to the front door while his thoughts wandered. He stretched his neck. Even beneath his outer jacket and suit jacket, the stiffness of his boiled white shirt and starched collar made him keep his back a bit straighter than normal.

Amy opened the door herself. She was wearing a purple dress. It had those sleeves with puffy tops that women liked. The puffy tops were decorated with purple velvet bows. The soft velvet was no match for how soft and lovely Amy's face looked to him. "You're beautiful."

Embarrassment at the bold way he'd blurted out his admiration melted away at her soft "Thank you" and the joyous look in her eyes.

Amy took a cape from the walnut shrank.

"Let me help you with that." Frank took the cape from her, and she turned her back to him. The cape was luxuriously thick and warm, the outer layer a deep shade of black velvet that seemed appropriate to protect someone as precious as Amy. A gentle floral scent wafted over him as he settled the cape on her shoulders. He wanted to enfold her in his arms but instead squeezed her shoulders lightly.

She tied the cape's satin ribbons at her throat, then picked up her hat from the marble-topped hall table and pinned it in place.

"You replaced the ribbons."

She turned to him with a smile. "You noticed."

"Would your father like to join us? I was thinking on the ride in that it's selfish of me to take you from him on Christmas Eve since you're his only family."

"How kind of you to ask. He's arranged to walk over with our neighbors, Roland's family, but would you mind if we sat with Father at the service? I've never attended a Christmas service without him."

"No, of course I don't mind."

The way her face shone was his reward. "He's upstairs. I'll just run and tell him we'll meet him at church."

Minutes later he helped her into the sleigh and climbed up beside her. As he lifted the reins, Amy laid one of her gloved hands over his and removed it in a quick gesture. "Please, may we talk for a minute before we leave?"

He turned his head to look at her, uncertainty making him hesitant, and nodded.

She clasped her hands in her lap. Her face was sober, and in the light of the lantern, he could see the seriousness in her eyes. "It's about the other night and the skating rink."

Somehow he'd known she'd wanted to speak about Walter. A burning started in his stomach. He waited for her to continue.

"When I told you I couldn't go skating with you because I was helping my father entertain a guest for dinner, I was telling the truth." Her words were coming in a rush. "After dinner Father asked me to go skating with Walter. I didn't want to, but I didn't know how to get out of it. I–I–It's important to me that you know I wasn't lying."

The weight that had sat on Frank's heart for days evaporated. "Thank you." The words sounded strangled. He cleared his throat and slapped the reins lightly. "Get up there, Gray."

The walks were full of people, swinging lanterns lighting their way. Sleighs passed in the streets. Smiles and greetings were on everyone's lips. Frank couldn't remember a time in his life when he'd been happier.

At the church he guided Gray into a long line of cutters. He took a wool blanket from the sleigh and covered Gray with it before helping Amy down.

When Amy took his arm and they walked into church together, Frank felt God had given him an incredible gift. They walked past the back pews where the high-school boys always sat and took a place in the wooden pew behind Jason and Pearl and the rest of Frank's family. When Amy's father sat down beside Amy, he and Frank shook hands solemnly.

Seated with Amy's shoulder against his, exchanging shy glances during the Christmas sermon and hymns, Frank realized the last year seemed a small time to pay for the joy of her presence. What would it be like to have her beside him like this for the rest of their lives? Could life possibly hold more for a man than that?

Thank You, Lord. Frank's heart ached with gratitude.

Sylvia and Roland stopped them on the way out of church. Curiosity shone bright in Sylvia's eyes as she looked from one to the other, but she didn't tease or ask questions about the two of them attending the service together. "A group of us are going caroling. You'll join us, won't you?"

Frank looked at Amy and raised his eyebrows. "Sounds like fun. Can you go?"

She turned to her father. "Do you mind?"

"Go along and have a nice time." Mr. Henderson waved his hands in a dismissing motion. "I'm stopping at the Reverend Conrad's open house for a bit."

"That's where the caroling will end up," Roland said.

Frank and Amy greeted and chatted with a number of friends before the caroling group headed out. "After all," Sylvia said, "someone has to get home from church before we start out so we'll have someone to sing for."

Snow was falling softly when they left the church. Amy smiled up at Frank. "It's perfect, isn't it? There's nothing more beautiful than an evening snowfall when there's no wind."

His hand covered hers where it rested on his arm, and he smiled down into her eyes. "Yes, it's perfect." Snowflakes caught on her lashes, and he wished he had the right to kiss those snowflakes away.

Frank checked on Gray before they left with the others. "It's not too cold. He should be all right."

For the next hour Frank and Amy laughed and sang praises with their friends and turned down numerous offers from those they caroled to enter their homes for cookies and cider. Frank wished the evening would never end.

The carolers chose a circular route and ended back at Rev. Conrad's home beside the darkened church.

Sylvia hurried in front of the others and held up mittened hands. "We simply must carol them before we go in."

Roland laughed. "Carol them? Those are the people we were singing with an hour ago."

Sylvia wrinkled her nose at him, bounced her hands as though conducting, and began singing. "Joy to the world—" The others joined in, including Roland, though he rolled his eyes at her.

Frank shared a laughing glance with Amy.

A movement, no more than a shadow on the snowy walk down the way, caught his attention. He recognized that weaving motion, the manner in which a man walked after he'd had too much to drink. Frank tried to dismiss the dread winding through him. Maybe the man would pass by without trying to join the group or sit down under a tree and watch the festivities in quiet.

The man staggered his way to the back of the group. Frank recognized him then. It was Tom, a balding bachelor in his forties, known more about town for his drinking than anything else. He stopped only a few feet from Frank and joined in the singing. The loud, off-tune, slurred words caused heads to swivel Tom's way. Seeing the new arrival, people shook their heads or rolled their eyes, some snickered, but no one quit singing.

Frank's heart went out to the man. He knew that Tom had no idea he was an object of ridicule. Tom was a quiet, retiring man when he was sober. A few drinks made it easier for him to be sociable, or what he considered sociable in his drunken state.

The parsonage door opened, and tall, slender, bearded Rev. Conrad and his pretty, round wife, Millicent, came out on the stoop. Guests crowded behind them. Light poured from the doorway in a golden path.

Frank liked the way the Reverend drew his wife close within his arm against the chill. Would he and Amy be like that one day, years of married life behind them and content in their life together? He hoped so.

Applause thanked the group when they were done, and Mrs. Conrad invited the carolers to join the guests. This time the group accepted.

Someone bumped against Frank and burped. A yeasty smell rose about them. "Excuse me."

Frank didn't need to look to know it was Tom, headed into the house with the others. Naturally he'd want to join in the festivities, and the drinks he'd had gave him the courage. Frank knew the Reverend and Mrs. Conrad and their guests wouldn't appreciate Tom in his inebriated state.

Frank saw the look of distaste in Amy's eyes as she watched Tom. With a sinking feeling, Frank realized he could have caused that look only a little over a year ago.

"Miss Amy," he said in a low voice, "I'm going to take Tom home. Will you wait here for me?"

She glanced from him to Tom and back again. "Yes."

Frank slipped an arm around Tom's shoulder. "Hi, Pal. Suppose we head back to your house and talk awhile?"

Tom shook his head. "I'm goin' in here. People to see."

"But there's important things I want to talk about with you."

"Important t'ings?" Tom's jaw hung so loose it almost waggled.

"Yes." Frank remembered from days standing at the bar beside Tom that Tom liked to talk about life and death and good and evil and all the subjects one might hear discussed in church, where Tom would never go to talk about them. "I have some thoughts on God and want to know what you think about them."

"Oh. A'right. Le's talk 'bout them inside." Tom took a step toward the door and would have fallen if Frank hadn't caught him. "Oops."

"Let's go to your place instead. It'll be hard to hear each other in there with all those people."

Tom frowned as though he wasn't certain whether or not to go along with Frank's proposal. He wasn't wearing a jacket. Frank removed his own and slipped it over Tom's shoulders, hoping it would be clean when he got it back.

Frank realized Amy was still beside them, though most everyone else had entered the house. "Go inside, Amy. Ask Roland if he'll help me out here."

Frank sighed deeply, watching her head toward the house. This wasn't the way he'd planned to spend this evening.

seven

Frank tried winding his muffler about his neck to ward off a bit of the cold that assailed him, keeping hold of Tom with one hand so the man didn't sink to the ground.

When Roland arrived, they managed between them to get Tom into Frank's sleigh, all the time Tom arguing he wanted to go to the preacher's house. Frank slid the buffalo lap robe over his shoulders and took up the reins.

Tom had stopped arguing by the time they reached his little log hut on the edge of town. He was almost asleep. Frank and Roland mostly carried him through the snow on the unshoveled path to the only door. The task was made more difficult because Roland also carried one of the sleigh lanterns.

Roland lifted the lantern high when they entered. "Whoa."

Frank stared in disbelief. There was barely room to walk in the one-room cabin. The floor, bed, only chair, and table were piled high with old papers, dirty used bean cans, rags, and bottles, most of them empty. The stove, which obviously served as both heating and cooking source, was cold. Roland set the lantern on top of it.

After Frank brushed a pile of stuff off the bed, he and Roland lowered Tom to the bed. It took a couple minutes to work Frank's coat off the man. Then they tugged the filthy blanket out from beneath Tom and laid it over him.

Roland propped his hands on his hips and looked around. "Merry Christmas, huh? No wonder he was headed to the preacher's house for some Christmas cheer."

"Or for food. I don't see any here."

Frank went outside to dig some wood from a snow-covered

woodpile. Back inside, he cleared rubbish away from the stove before starting a fire. "This place is a fire trap."

Unable to do anything else for Tom, Frank and Roland headed back to the party. Frank wondered how long they'd been away. Would Amy be impatient over his absence? Frank grimaced. It was probably Mr. Henderson who was impatient, thinking Frank wasn't treating his daughter well.

As soon as they entered the house, Frank began searching for Amy. She wasn't easy to find. People of all ages and sizes filled the parsonage. Women stood about the dining-room table, discussing whose *krumkake* was crispest, whose sugar cookies thinnest, and whose fruitcake had the most fruit. The men gathered in the parlor, seated on the horsehair sofa, or one of the parlor chairs that had been drawn into a circle, discussed the silver situation and whether the coming year would bring relief from the economic depression; as well as the latest gossip that the saloon keeper had lost control of his horses the night before, causing man and beast to tumble down the riverbank. Boys chased each other about, darting in and out of the adults with barely more than a "Yes, Mother" over their shoulders when reprimanded. Girls stood or sat self-consciously straight and ate daintily from china plates filled with cookies.

Frank was wondering whether Amy had gone home when he heard her voice at his side. "Would you like some cider?"

"Thanks." He accepted the warm apple cider, spiced with cloves and cinnamon sticks. "I'm sorry I was gone so long."

"It was kind of you to help him home."

"It seemed like the thing to do at the time, but I should probably have asked someone else to take him. I didn't mean to run out on you."

"I know that."

Her understanding calmed his worry.

Frank usually preferred to sit on the sidelines and observe

others socializing, but with Amy at his side, the gathering was a completely different experience for him. He loved the way Amy's glance darted to his to share something someone said or a child's antics. He loved the way people spoke to them as though they were one. He loved the way Amy's hand remained snug within his arm as they moved about, visiting with various friends.

He stopped beside an old gentleman seated in a plush chair in the parlor. The man's hands were folded over the top of a cane, which he held between his legs. Frank laid a hand on the man's shoulder. Leaning down so his lips were close to the man's ears, he said, "It's Frank Sterling, Mr. Sutter. Merry Christmas."

The man lifted a face with clouded eyes and smiled an almost toothless greeting. "Hullo there, young man."

Amy touched one of her hands lightly to one of his. "Merry Christmas, Mr. Sutter. It's Amy Henderson. You remember me, don't you?"

Frank was glad to see she greeted the old man so sweetly.

" 'Course I remember you," Mr. Sutter sputtered. "You two sweet on each other now?" He cackled at his own audacity.

Frank's embarrassment was lost in his laugh when he heard Amy's surprised giggle. "I'm working on her, Mr. Sutter, that I am," he admitted and grinned at the shy dropping of Amy's lashes.

They listened for a few minutes as Mr. Sutter, one of the town's first settlers, spoke of early Christmases in Chippewa City.

"You must miss those days," Amy said when he paused.

"What I miss most is my wife, and a close second is her Christmas bread. She made the best *julekage* on the prairie." Sutter smacked his lips.

Frank and Amy erupted into laughter once more. *I'm glad we're at the beginning of our romance and not looking back on its ending,* Frank thought.

Mr. Henderson was still at the parsonage, as were Jason and Pearl. Frank and Amy spoke with them all. Frank's arm felt empty when Amy and Pearl went off to the kitchen to locate some *julekage* for Mr. Sutter.

"We're over here," Jason reminded him dryly, digging his elbow into Frank's ribs.

Frank pulled his gaze back from the kitchen doorway with an embarrassed start.

Roland chuckled. "Looks like you've got it bad, old man."

Frank only smiled. "Having it bad" felt awfully good.

Roland frowned at his cup of cider. He opened his jacket, and Frank saw the top of a bottle. "Either of you want to add a pinch of something stronger to this?" Roland raised his eyebrows.

"No." Jason's voice was low but cracked with anger. "And this isn't the place for such shenanigans."

Roland held up a hand as if to fend Jason off. "I'm not looking to cause trouble. Just thought a bit of the cup that cheers seemed in line with celebrating." He shot a glance at Frank.

"Did you get that at Tom's place?"

"Figured he'll never miss it."

"That's stealing."

Roland leaned closer to Frank. "You used to be a lot more fun," he said before he turned away.

Frank and Jason watched him cross the room and slap an academy friend on the back. "Think he'll find anyone to share his bounty with here?" Jason asked.

"Probably. Isn't too hard. Usually people find you." Frank remembered all too well how easy it was to identify those who might carry a flask they were willing to share.

A moment later Amy and Pearl rejoined Jason and Frank, and thoughts of liquor were drowned in pleasant companionship.

When another couple claimed Jason and Pearl's attention,

Amy said, "I should probably leave soon. Father left a few minutes ago. I hate for him to be alone on Christmas."

Immediately Frank went in search of Amy's cape and his jacket. He hated to think of this evening ending, but he still had the ride home with Amy to look forward to.

He stopped to speak with Rev. Conrad, in a few private words explaining the condition of Tom's cabin and his lack of provisions. He was relieved when the pastor promised to stop and check on Tom and bring him some food later.

When Frank returned to the parlor with their outer garments, his gaze searched for Amy. He stopped abruptly when he saw Walter Bay speaking to her. From the tight way she held her shoulders and chin, she wasn't too happy with him.

Frank made his way through the thinning crowd. "Here's your cape, Amy." He nodded at Walter. "Hope you're having a nice Christmas."

Walter slid a thumb beneath the watch chain strung across his vest. "Not so good so far, but it will get better. Wish I could say the same for yours." With a grin, he turned and walked away.

Frank held Amy's cape for her. "What was that cryptic statement supposed to mean?"

"He just likes to spread unhappiness," she said quietly.

"Nothing could make me unhappy tonight," he whispered.

Frank thought he saw the glint of tears in her eyes. From joy? Was she as happy as he to be together? If the tears were real, they only lasted a moment.

Outside, a soft hiss sounded when Frank lit the lanterns on each side of the cutter. Vapors from the sulfur and kerosene blended with the fresh smell of falling snow before he slid the glass down to protect the flame. He helped Amy onto the leather seat and tucked the buffalo robe about her. "I'm afraid the brick is cold by now, but maybe this will keep you warm."

Her sweet smile thanked him.

He brushed snow from Gray's blanket before climbing up beside Amy. "Do you want to head straight home, or do we have time to take Gray for a trot along the river?"

"A ride along the river would be lovely, if we don't take too long."

Clouds hid the moon and stars, but the sleigh's lanterns provided more than enough light combined with the yellow patches of lamplight falling from windows in every home they passed. Frank took the hill road that wound down from the residential area on the prairie to river level, talking softly to Gray while guiding him down the steep incline. He'd take no chance on a runaway sleigh with Amy in it.

Globe-topped streetlights cast their beams on the couple as the cutter slid down Main Street. Frank urged Gray into a trot. The street was popular with sleighers in the evenings, when most businesses were closed and there were no pedestrians or horses to endanger. Frank and Amy waved and exchanged calls of "Merry Christmas" as they passed other sleighs.

Frank pointed out a dark, quiet saloon to Amy. It was closed for the night out of respect for Christ's birth. "I know a couple men besides Tom who are likely spending tonight in their rooms alone with a hoarded bottle."

"Wouldn't they have attended church? Almost everyone goes on Christmas Eve, even if they avoid it the rest of the year."

"These men wouldn't feel at ease in a church. The camaraderie of the saloons is the closest thing they know to a home." His heart hurt for them, especially Tom, and he sent up a silent prayer that the Lord would be with them tonight, even if they hadn't made the move to join others in worshiping Him.

"You used to drink, and you weren't like that."

He didn't hear condemnation in Amy's comment, only confusion. "I might have ended up just like them."

"But you didn't." She slipped one of her hands over one of his. "I knew you wouldn't."

"It's not so easy, Amy. People think a man can just say he's not going to drink anymore, that he can see it's hurting him and the people who care for him, and just stop. It's not that easy."

"I wish I understood better; truly I do."

It was a difficult thing for him to talk about. Just to think of sharing with her how rough it was to stop drinking scared him, made him feel. . .vulnerable. What if she thought less of him because he wasn't an iron-willed man? But if they were going to have any chance together, they had to be honest with each other.

"Your prayers helped me, and your faith in me, but it was still hard. A lot harder than I thought it would be when I told God I was quitting. If I'd been drinking as long as some of these men, I don't know if I would have made it. During the time I was frequenting the saloons, I got to know the men people call the town drunks." Memories drifted before his eyes, and sadness welled up within him like a wave.

He realized Amy was waiting for him to continue. He had to clear his throat before he could say, "Some of them have awful, painful things to forget or live with, Amy. They aren't terrible, lazy people the way town folks say. They're just people who hurt something fierce inside."

"How can we help them, Frank?"

"I guess the place to start is to remember they aren't the alcohol. Beneath the people we think we see are souls God made in His image. Souls He loves—loves as much as He loves anyone else. If we can remember that when we pray for them, maybe we can learn how to help them."

"I'll try to remember, and I'll pray."

If they hadn't been on Main Street, he would have hugged her then and there.

He'd been on his way to a lonely life with liquor for his best friend when he'd made the decision a year ago to turn his life over to God. But for that choice, Amy wouldn't be beside him now, her shoulder bumping companionably against his, her perfume bringing springtime into the winter air. Without the promise of Amy's companionship, would he have had the strength to change his life? He doubted it. *Thank You, Lord,* he repeated for the dozenth time that night.

The sleigh slid onto the mill bridge, and they looked down on Shakespearean Rink. Laughter drifted up to them from the few brave souls gliding over the ice. "I want to skate with you again, Amy."

She smiled up at him. "That would be lovely."

He slid one arm a bit stiffly around her shoulders as they moved off the bridge. It could be dangerous to drive with only one hand about the reins, but Frank felt Gray was trustworthy and gentle. More dangerous was the chance Amy would tell him to remove his arm. She didn't, instead relaxing against him, sending his heart into a pounding rhythm.

The road was a popular spot for sleigh races, but tonight there weren't many other sleighs since the moon wasn't lighting the road. Bare-branched cottonwoods stood sentinel along the river. The sleigh bells chimed saucily above the *sh-sh-sh* of the sleigh runners.

"We'd better turn back. I thought there'd be more people out tonight. I don't want to damage your reputation."

Frank needed both hands to turn Gray and the sleigh back toward town. Then he urged Gray to a stop. He slid his arm back around Amy's shoulders and risked pulling her close in a gentle hug. Wonder wrapped around his heart at the trusting way she relaxed into his embrace.

He breathed in the sweet scent that lingered about her soft hair, then touched his lips to her neck, at that place just below the dainty, purple stones that dangled from her ear. He drew his head back slightly and, barely breathing, kissed her lips. "Amy, you are so precious," he whispered, then met her warm lips again. She surrendered a kiss so sweet his chest ached.

And finally he kissed the snowflakes off her lashes.

"We'd better get home," he repeated.

Amy's head rested against his shoulder as he drove. To Frank it seemed love enclosed them in a circle so strong it was tangible.

At the mill bridge where the streetlights again brightened the way, Amy lifted her head from his shoulder with a sigh. Frank turned to smile at her, and the feathers on her hat tickled his nose, causing them both to laugh. Such a little thing to cause him so much joy, but it did.

He applied both hands to the reins again, not wishing to embarrass Amy by a public display of their affection as they drove through town. After pulling up in front of her home, he took a decorated box from behind the seat and held it out to her.

Her eyes widened. Her gaze moved from the box to his eyes. "A gift?" She didn't take it from him.

"It's probably a breach of manners to give you a Christmas gift when we're only beginning to court, but I thought of you as soon as I saw this and wanted you to have it. If you say I must take it back, I will, but I hope you'll keep it."

Amy took it from him then. "I haven't anything for you," she said, opening the box.

"You gave me tonight."

The look in her eyes was gift enough to last him a hundred Christmases.

"Oh, Frank!" Amy pulled the gift from layers of tissue. A man and woman skated together in a glass globe on a walnut stand. "I saw this in the jewelry-store window and fell in love with it at first sight." Her eyes shined with joy. "I shall treasure it."

Her gladness warmed him.

They walked up to the house slowly. Frank hoped Amy

was savoring their last minutes together as he was.

"I suppose your father is waiting for you," Frank said, looking at the lace-framed parlor window that looked out on the front porch.

"Yes. He always waits up for me, even when I'm at a house party with girlfriends. He says he worries about me more than most parents since we lost Mother."

At the door Frank lifted one of Amy's gloved hands to his lips, wishing fervently etiquette and the possibility of gossiping neighbors allowed him greater liberties. "Good night, Amy."

He started to release her hand, but she held on. "Frank. . ."

"Yes?"

"I'm so proud and glad for you that you've kept your promise to God to give up drinking. You won't change your mind, will you? No matter what?"

The urgency underscoring her words amused him. "No, Amy, I won't change my mind, no matter what." He kissed the back of her hand again and gave it a gentle squeeze. "Blessed Christmas, Amy."

"Blessed Christmas, Frank."

The snow stopped before he and Gray reached the edge of town. The livery owner had asked Frank to wait until Christmas Day to return the horse and sleigh. Gray's hooves thudded softly on the snow-padded roadway. Only a dusting had fallen, not enough to dangerously obscure the edge of the road, for which Frank was grateful. His thoughts weren't on driving but on Amy.

When the door to her house had opened, the light from the lamp on the hall table had spilled out. He'd thought for a moment he'd seen tears glittering in her eyes again. He'd always pictured Amy as a strong woman, not the type who cried easily. If he had seen tears in her eyes, he hoped they were tears of joy because the two of them were finally together.

"Blessed Christmas, Amy," he whispered again into the prairie night.

❧

Amy slipped the nightgown over her head. The rose-sprigged flannel fell to her toes in soft, comforting warmth. She sat down on the bench in front of her vanity and began brushing the hair that fell in rippling waves to her waist.

Her gaze wasn't on her mirror image but on the snow globe that sat on a lace doily on the vanity. She turned the key on the walnut base, and the couple twirled to a waltz. Amy's eyes misted over until the man and woman were only a haze.

"I should have told him." Reliving Frank's kisses, his endearments, she knew she should feel guilty, but she didn't. *It might be wrong to want this night to remember, Lord, but I do. This one night is all Frank and I will ever have together.*

She knew it was wrong to allow him to hold her, to kiss her, to believe they would continue courting. Before Frank had arrived, she'd promised herself she'd tell him right after the church service about her agreement with Walter. But then they'd gone caroling and to the open house. The opportunity presented itself in the sleigh when they left the parson's, but by then the temptation was too great.

"Frank has such a beautiful heart, Lord." Watching him with Tom and later with Mr. Sutter, she couldn't help comparing Frank's compassionate nature with cynical Walter. Her heart cried out for the love of a gentle yet strong man like Frank.

"This night has to last us forever, Lord," she reminded herself and God, trying to assuage her guilt.

Amy moved the snow globe to the bedside table, where she could watch the couple turn in the moonlight that was breaking through the clouds. She climbed into bed, pulled the pink satin comforter over her shoulders, and fell asleep in the memory of Frank's embrace.

The first thing she saw the next morning was the skaters. She smiled and snuggled further into the covers, closing her eyes and reliving Frank's kisses.

She ignored the knock at her bedroom door until it was followed by her father's boisterous, "Merry Christmas, Amy."

She leaped out of bed. How could she have forgotten the Christmas-morning rituals? "I'll be downstairs in a few minutes, Father."

Christmas breakfast and the exchange of gifts were a bittersweet time as always since her mother died. The day passed quickly and pleasantly with neighbors dropping in to visit and she and her father visiting others. Amy loved the way everyone opened their homes on Christmas Eve and Christmas Day. It made the whole town feel like family. At one point she found herself daydreaming what it might be like for her and Frank to welcome visitors some future Christmas. She closed the door firmly on that dream, remembering with whom she had promised to spend her future.

It was late afternoon when she turned from greeting the editor of the local paper and his wife to see Walter enter the parlor. Amy stumbled in her words so badly that the editor's wife looked to see what had caught the younger woman's attention.

Amy tried to recover the situation. She smiled at the couple. "I see we have more company. Will you excuse me? I must see whether the refreshments are adequate."

She picked up a crystal plate still half-filled with sugar cookies and headed toward the kitchen, hoping for a few more minutes of respite before speaking with Walter.

"May I help you with that?" Walter took the plate from her hands.

Too late. Amy bit back a groan.

"You do look lovely in that blue gown, my dear."

Amy's face heated. She glanced about quickly to see who

might be near. "Don't call me by endearments." She kept her voice low.

Walter laughed, and her indignation increased. She swept through the swinging door into the kitchen. Walter followed. She tried to ignore him while refilling the plate. At least this room was empty of people. Mrs. Jorgenson had the day off to spend with her family.

Walter caught Amy's wrist in a tight grip. "You haven't forgotten our agreement, have you? I expect you to act in public as if you like me, and more than a little bit."

She looked pointedly at her wrist until he dropped it. Tossing her head, she challenged, "Why do you want me for your wife? Why not a woman who loves you and wants you as dearly as you want her?"

He chuckled. "What's the challenge in that?" He placed his hands on the counter on each side of her, trapping her. "Let's announce our engagement now, here." He gestured toward the parlor with his head. "Or rather, in there."

She pushed at one of his hands. "I need to get some cookies from the jars on the table."

He released her and leaned back against the counter. "I'm waiting for your agreement."

Agreement, not answer. She busied herself with the cookies, her back to him. Her mind darted about for a way to postpone the dreaded time. "Don't you want a special party to announce it? An engagement party? That way you can invite everyone with whom you want to share the news. This way it will only be announced to whoever happens to have dropped in for a few minutes."

"I like the gathered crowd. The editor of the paper is here. He'll be sure to include the announcement in this week's news."

"I should think a man of your importance in the community would want the announcement to be made in the proper manner."

She heard his step. Then his hands at her waist made her gasp. All too close to her ear, she heard him say, "Surely a happy bridegroom-to-be can be forgiven for announcing the joyful news a bit, shall we say, out of step with conventional demand?"

"Unhand me."

Laughing, he released her. "You are a spirited lass. I'm delighted. I thought you were one of those women who corseted her mind and emotions as well as her body."

His coarse words revolted her. "If you find me so lacking in agreeable attributes, why demand I marry you?"

He spread his hands wide. "You're the daughter of the most admired man in this part of the prairie."

"Admired but poor."

"People don't know that, and they needn't if you keep your part of the bargain."

"I'm not likely to back out, considering the cost." She turned about with the replenished plate of cookies. "Unless you have something more to say, I'm going back to the parlor."

He followed on her heels. *Like a stray dog one can't discourage,* she thought in annoyance.

When they entered the room, her father beamed and reached for a cookie. "I was wondering where those went."

Amy smiled at him with warm affection as she set the plate down. "You would have found your way to them in the kitchen before long, I suspect."

Polite and friendly laughter from gathered guests greeted her remark.

Walter rubbed his palms together briskly. "Mr. Henderson, I have wonderful news." He reached for Amy's elbow and drew her beside him, grinning down at her.

Lord, I'm not ready for this. Please, please find a way to stop it. Her gaze remained fixed on Walter's, everything within her pleading for release from her promise.

The crowd watched them. No one moved. It seemed to Amy no one even breathed.

Mr. Henderson broke the stillness. "What is this wonderful news, Mr. Bay?"

There was no release. Walter's fingers pinched her arm as if to remind her not to deny his words. "Your daughter just agreed to marry me."

"Amy!" Frank's voice filtered through the crowd's murmurs and surprised congratulations.

Amy turned toward the sound. Frank stood in the parlor doorway, his face ashen, his eyes black with pain and shock. *No!* her heart screamed. She took a step toward him but was stopped by Walter's hold.

"The little woman is surprised." She heard the challenge underscoring Walter's words. "She didn't think I'd have the courage to announce it right away like this, did you, Dear?"

"No. No, I didn't."

Frank stepped back. A moment later the front door slammed. It reverberated through her as Walter's announcement had reverberated through her life, crashing her world apart.

eight

The grandfather clock in the hall struck seven as Amy dropped into the satin-covered parlor chair and rested her feet on the tiny footstool. Walter had stayed until after the last guest left. Finally he left also. She felt as limp as a linen gown in a rainstorm.

She glanced down at her left hand resting on the arm of the chair. A square emerald blinked back at her from her ring finger. It felt heavy and awkward. *I hadn't thought I'd ever hate a piece of jewelry.*

Her father sat down on the couch with a sigh. He studied the crystal plate of cookies on the tea table in front of him as though it were a chessboard. He finally selected a date-filled delicacy and sat back. "I'm glad the guests left us a few cookies to enjoy."

Amy managed a tiny smile. "If they hadn't, I'm sure Mrs. Jorgenson would have made more for us."

"Yes. What would we do without her?"

His comment required no answer. She felt him watching her as he ate, but she kept her gaze carefully away from him. She was sure later she would cry, but for the moment it was all too new, too much to absorb that Walter had walked into her house and destroyed her happiness, her hopes, her life.

She felt like she had when her mother died. She hated that anything would compare to that grief, but it was so. Every part of her insides burned. When she remembered Frank's eyes, the betrayal in them, her betrayal of him—how was she going to live with that memory for the rest of her life?

Her father brushed crumbs from his hands. "Are you going

74

to tell me what it's all about?"

"What do you mean?" She continued to avoid his eyes.

"You know what I mean. You and Walter."

Amy forced a smile. The happy bride-to-be. It was important she remember to play the role properly if she didn't want him to guess the reason for the marriage. She held up her left hand. "I thought we made it quite clear. We're to be married."

"A week ago I couldn't convince you he was worth considering as a husband."

"A lot can happen in a week." Could it ever. "We'd had a disagreement."

"When? About what?"

"At the Windom Academy Christmas party. It was a petty argument. It's not important." They'd disagreed in spirit if not in words.

"Seems a bit unusual that you spent last night with young Sterling and today you announce your engagement to Bay."

Amy smoothed a fold in her skirt's lace insert. "I was keeping my promise to Mr. Sterling."

"Is that all last night was, keeping a promise?"

She nodded.

"You seemed to be enjoying yourself, keeping that promise."

"Of course I did. We were among friends."

"And you had given young Sterling your word."

"Yes."

"It's not like you to make an important decision like this so quickly, Amy, and without discussing it with me."

She looked at him then, raising her eyebrows, trying to put surprise into her expression. "Didn't Walter ask you for my hand, Father?"

"No."

"It's surprising he didn't ask you for my hand, or for permission to ask for my hand, don't you think? He does like people to believe he conducts himself properly."

Mr. Henderson leaned forward, rested his forearms on his knees, and stared hard at her. "You're not overflowing with joy over your betrothal."

"Wait until I buy my trousseau." This time her grin was real. They both knew how she loved new clothes. Then she remembered they were living on borrowed money. There weren't funds for a trousseau.

Her father's answering grin didn't hint at his financial truth. "Now you sound like yourself."

Amy went to him and kissed him on the forehead. "I guess the excitement of Christmas and the engagement has worn me out. I'll be my usual chipper self tomorrow, you'll see."

But as she walked up the broad stairway to her bedroom, the knowledge they were both living lies weighed down her spirit. Her father lived the lie that he was wealthy instead of bankrupt. She lived the lie that she was happy to be engaged to Walter. A week ago she wouldn't have thought it possible they would ever lie to each other.

Frank believed she'd lied to him, too, through her actions last night. And hadn't she? She'd thought only of herself when she took his kiss and embrace for her memories. If only she'd had the courage to tell him the awful truth.

If she'd told him the truth, she would have saved herself, too, for she'd felt his arms about her every moment today. "I always will; I know it."

She yanked off the emerald ring, dropped it carelessly into the top vanity drawer, and slammed the drawer shut, glad to hide from sight the reminder that she'd bound herself to Walter.

❧

Frank pitched the forkful of old hay out the calf-barn door into the wagon bed. Frustration and anger put more strength than necessary behind the pitch. The barn didn't need to be cleaned, but he had to do something, or he wouldn't be able to bear just being alive, and he didn't want to be with people.

"What's gotten into you?" Jason had demanded at breakfast.

Frank hadn't answered. He couldn't make the words form, the words that said Amy was engaged to Walter Bay. He'd pushed back his chair and headed for the barn, the place where he always went when he was hurting—out to the animals he loved and the familiar scents of straw and warm animals.

A cat rubbed against his leg. "Meow."

Frank bent to pet its golden back. "Watch yourself, Gideon. I wouldn't want you tossed out." Gideon never did have sense enough to stay away from dangerous things like pitchforks.

"Would have thought you'd learned your lesson when you lost your eye." Frank recalled finding the six-week-old kitten in the hay in the cow barn, one of its eyes lacerated and infected. He'd ached for the kitten that he knew couldn't survive. There wasn't extra money for the veterinarian to help farm cats. Cats were easily and cheaply replaced.

For some reason, this little guy hadn't seemed ready to give in to what everyone thought was inevitable. So Frank had asked Pearl's father, Dr. Matt, if he'd try to help the cat. The kind man had agreed. The eye couldn't be saved, so it had been removed to keep the infection from spreading. The kitten had taken the adjustment to one eye in stride. Its courage seemed larger than its size and earned it the name Gideon, after the tough little leader in the Old Testament.

Frank's brothers had teased him for going to so much trouble for a barn cat, but Frank didn't let that bother him. Gideon seemed to realize Frank had saved his life. He followed Frank around like a dog and snuggled against Frank whenever the opportunity presented itself, purring in pleasure.

"You trust I'm always going to see you in time to keep from hurting you, don't you, Pal?" He pushed the cat gently away. "I wouldn't hurt you on purpose, but it could happen, all the same."

Amy hurt me on purpose.

"Think about something else," he commanded himself. "Think about Tom. There's someone who's worse off than you." Or maybe not. Was there a woman in Tom's past who'd betrayed him? If so, he'd never confided it to Frank in the nights they'd drunk together. Not that he remembered, anyway.

He should probably check on Tom again, make sure he hadn't gone through all the food he'd brought him on Christmas Day. Rev. Conrad had stopped by Tom's sometime between the open house on Christmas Eve and the time Frank had arrived. He'd left some bread and Christmas baked goods and a Bible. Frank could see there'd been an attempt to pick up the place a bit. He knew that wouldn't last.

When he'd left Tom's place, he'd swung past Amy's, hoping to talk her into another sleigh ride before he returned the cutter to the livery stable. He'd known as soon as he stopped that the sleigh ride was out. Amy wouldn't be so impolite as to leave her guests. But he'd thought he might say hello.

He hadn't said hello, but she'd found a mighty powerful way to say good-bye.

Back to Amy again. Couldn't even trust his own thoughts.

He threw all his muscles behind his work. Toss a pile of old straw. *She lied to me.* Another forkload. Toss it. *She betrayed me.* Another forkload. *She promised to marry Walter Bay only hours after kissing me.*

"Why didn't she tell me she was in love with him?" he asked himself for the umpteenth time. There could be only one answer. She wasn't the woman he'd believed.

He'd thought she was as beautiful in spirit as in face: sweet, honest, strong, the true-through-and-through kind of woman.

She'd taken him for a ride. Trotted him about in front of the whole town Christmas Eve and the next day announced her engagement to Walter.

"I gave her the chance to back out, told her she didn't need to keep her promise to go to church with me Christmas Eve.

So why did she? And why, above all, did she act as though she cared, even letting me kiss her?"

Because she does care for me. The words whispered through his mind.

"Fool." He stuffed the pitchfork in the straw. Sinking to the floor, he buried his head in his hands. No matter that truth showed itself in her indelicate, unfeeling actions, his heart believed in her. He felt bruised inside; every inch of him felt bruised. The pain hadn't let up for one waking moment since he'd heard Walter utter the words that changed his life: "Your daughter just agreed to marry me."

A few drinks would erase the pain—for awhile. He could easily hide a bottle out here in the barn. No one would be the wiser. He could tell Jason he was going out for a last check on the cattle at night, dig out his bottle, and on to bed. No more tossing and turning. No dreams. No images of Amy and Walter flooding his mind. For a few hours he'd be free of it all. It would be so easy.

It would destroy him, destroy his self-respect.

He wrapped his arms around his middle and bent into the pain. "Help me, Lord."

nine

Three days later Frank turned from pulping turnips and carrots to add to the cows' feed when Jason entered the barn. "Get the town errands done?"

"Yes." Jason frowned at the floor.

Frank straightened, a carrot in one hand, and stared at him. "Something wrong? Didn't the implement shop have the parts we need to repair the harrow plow?"

"No, but they'll have them in a few weeks."

"Shouldn't be a problem. Winter won't be over for a bit yet." He grinned.

Jason stuffed his hands in his trouser pockets. "I heard about. . .about Amy and Walter."

Frank felt like he'd been kicked in the gut. He couldn't get his breath. He turned his back to his brother. Why was he so stunned? He'd known it was only a matter of time before the family found out. He tried to speak, but a sob rose up in his throat instead.

"I'm sorry, Frank. If you want to talk about it, well, I'm around."

Frank nodded, struggling to keep the sobs within. Jason's hand patted his shoulder, and then Jason's footsteps could be heard through the straw. A rush of cold air swept over Frank as the door squeaked open and shut.

The sobs rolled out. Frank leaned against a post, helpless against the sorrow pouring from him. *Not again. I can't endure this. I just can't keep enduring this.*

No one in the family said anything to Frank about Amy after Jason's comment. Frank was sure Jason had told them not to. The lack of words didn't stem the pity in his family's eyes. Frank hated that his torn soul hung bare before them.

He arose before the rest of the family each morning and escaped to the barns or the work shed. There was always plenty to keep him busy. He needn't bother with clean clothes or shaving. The cows, hogs, cats, and dogs kept him company without feeling sorry for him. They let him talk all he wanted about Amy without offering unwanted advice. When he cried, the cats and dogs snuggled close and offered love. At night Frank waited until the farmhouse windows darkened before heading home to bed.

He could see the worry in Jason's face when they met while going about chores. Did Jason think he was drinking again? If so, he didn't say so. Frank hoped it was only the state of his heart that concerned his brother.

At dusk on New Year's Eve, Jason and Frank occupied their normal station on the wooden T-stools, milking cows. Kerosene lamps hung safely above them. As usual since the news about Amy, there was none of the singing or whistling they occasionally indulged in to shorten the chore. Black-and-white and tabby cats sat in the straw, watching and waiting. Milk hissed into the pails. In the cold evening air the cow's udders provided welcome warmth to Frank's hands.

"I'm done." Jason stood beside him, T-stool in one hand and milk pail in the other. "I'll start the separating while you finish milking Sudsy here."

"All right. I'm only half done milking her."

A couple minutes later Frank heard the milk being poured into the metal separator, though the cow stood between him and Jason.

"You haven't forgotten it's New Year's Eve, have you, Frank?"

"Nope."

"Are you going to the watch party and prayer service with us? The kids spent all afternoon shelling corn to pop."

Frank rested his head against Sudsy's huge, warm side. "Don't think I'll go. I'm pretty tired." He'd been tired unto exhaustion since Walter Bay announced his "wonderful news."

"Aw, Sudsy, no." He shook his head in disgust. "This pail of milk won't be going through the separator, Jason. Sudsy stepped in it."

Jason chuckled. "Oh, well. The cows need to be milked, whether the milk goes to us or the cats."

"I'll finish separating the milk and cream and clean the separator. You go on. The family will be waiting for you to clean up so they can leave."

"Are you sure?"

"I'm sure."

There was a pause. "I can stick around tonight if you want."

"I'll be fine. The Lord isn't stuck in the church. I'm not ready to face everyone yet."

He could almost hear Jason protesting in the stillness. Finally Jason spoke. "You'll have to get back to living sometime."

"I know." Frank didn't know anything of the kind, but it didn't seem worth arguing about. Nothing seemed worth that much effort anymore.

He waited until the family left before going into the house. It was nice to have it to himself for a change, at least at first. He supposed he should take advantage of the privacy—heat some water and take a bath—but that took so much work. He changed out of chore clothes, giving himself a lick-and-a-promise sponge bath, then settled in the rocking chair beside the kitchen stove. No sense building a fire in the parlor stove for one person. Besides, the picture Amy painted last year of Pearl and Jason hung above the sofa. He didn't need yet another reminder of her.

He opened up *The Old Farmer's Almanac* for 1895. A new year. A year he'd looked forward to like no other. What a way to start it. Instead of beginning a romance, he was more alone than he'd ever been in his life.

Jason was right, even though he'd stated it wrong. It was time to return to normal life.

Frank banked the fire in the stove and put out the lamps. Then he saddled up his horse and headed for town.

He hadn't a lantern, but moonlight on the snow lit the way. Others traveled the road, mostly headed to town for church or New Year's parties. A couple of young men from the Academy raced their cutters, sleigh bells sending a merry tune not at all in keeping with Frank's mood. He greeted people with a nod or a touch to his hat.

Sleighs, wagonsleds, and horses lined the side of the street near the church. Lanterns beside the door lit the front steps for parishioners. Sleighs were pulling up near the steps, dropping off ladies.

Frank reined in his horse at the end of the line. He hadn't dressed for church, wasn't even certain when he started out that he was headed for church, but it was the safest place for him in his present state of mind. Maybe no one would notice or recognize him if he slipped into one of the back pews.

He dismounted, tied his horse to the post, and started up the walk. The sight of Amy and Walter climbing the church steps brought him up short.

Frank spun around and stalked back to his horse, ignoring the greetings of others on the path. Once in the saddle, he barely paid attention to where he headed. Tears blurred his vision. He needed to get away, and any direction would do. The fewer people around, the better.

The downtown streets stood empty because only the skating rink, billiard halls, and saloons were open. He tied his horse in front of Plummer's Saloon. The promises he'd made to himself and Amy shouted in his head for attention. He tried to shut them out. He only wanted one night without the pain, without the ache that had filled him for the last week, without the memories. Was that such a terrible thing?

Once inside, he didn't hesitate. He strode right to the bar. Tables and chairs were outlawed in saloons in Chippewa City since the gambling-den raid above this very saloon last year, but the town fathers and the Temperance League were mistaken if they thought that kept men standing while they drank. Men seated on the floor rested their backs against the walls or bar.

A bartender in a white shirt with colorful garters greeted him with a pleasant smile. "What's your pleasure, Sir?"

"Rye."

Frank pulled off his gloves and tossed them on the counter. The place was the same as he remembered. The familiarity settled upon him like a comfortable old coat: the yeasty odor, the sounds of glasses clinking, of laughter a bit too high and too bright, of beer *glug-glugging* into glasses.

Another patron leaned on the bartender's shoulder and bent his ear, delaying Frank's drink. Frank, impatient, looked about while he waited.

Old Tom slumped in a corner. An open glass lay on the floor beside his hand. His mouth hung open. His eyes were closed. Frank figured he was asleep or, more accurately, passed out. Frank envied him. *That's where I'm headed, beyond caring about this world.*

He looked again for the bartender and caught sight of his own image in the mirror on the wall behind the bar. He barely recognized himself. Circles underscored his eyes. His normally neatly-trimmed mustache was overgrown into the scraggly beard covering his cheeks and chin.

And to think he'd almost attended church this way. His appearance would have shocked Amy. He snorted. An adverse sense of pleasure stole through him at the thought. If she saw him looking like this, maybe she'd realize how much she'd hurt him.

The bartender set a glass in front of him. "Sorry it took me so long."

Frank picked up the glass and held it near his face, smelling the amber liquid. When Amy heard he'd started drinking again, she'd know he started because he cared for her so much. Then she'd feel guilty for the way she'd treated him.

Your promise wasn't to Amy.

The words sounded in his mind as clearly as if spoken. He set the glass down with a *thunk*. Of course his promise had been to Amy, to her and her father. He'd promised he wouldn't drink or gamble for a year.

No. That wasn't quite right. He'd decided to follow Christ. As part of that decision, he'd given up drinking and gambling, but he couldn't have followed up on changing those habits if it weren't for the promise that Christ loved him and stood by him through everything.

The year was a guarantee, a show of good faith to Amy's father that Frank was serious about his commitment to the Lord. Maybe it was that year that cost him the chance to win Amy by allowing Walter Bay to win her heart, but the Lord hadn't broken any of His promises to Frank.

It still hurt, losing faith in Amy's goodness, losing the chance to win her. Walking through fire couldn't hurt any more than losing her.

He looked down at the drink still in his hand. A few of these and that pain would be gone for awhile. This glass would start it, take the edge off, give his brain that fuzzy-edged feeling.

He glanced at Tom. *I want to be as free of pain as he is at this moment, but if I let myself do this tonight, the pain will be back in the morning. I'll have to do this again and again and again until there's no stopping between drinks.*

His hand tightened on the glass. Sweat trickled out from under his hat. Without drinking, his only choice was to live with the pain. Why didn't God take the pain away so he didn't have to fight this battle?

He'll help you live through the pain, so you don't need to give up everything else good in your life to escape the pain.

He did have good things in his life: his family, the animals he loved, the academy.

Frank pulled some coins from his trouser pocket and tossed them on the counter. He took out a couple silver dollars and added them to the coins. "Make sure someone gets Old Tom home safe and sound when you close up, all right?"

"Sure thing," the bartender agreed.

"One more thing." Frank shoved the glass of untouched rye toward the barkeep. "Throw this away."

He walked out feeling taller than he had in days.

ten

Amy stood back, hands on her hips, and studied the oil paintings on the wall of the Academy hall. They looked as though they hung evenly, all but the one of Pearl standing on the farmstead porch, watching for Jason. That one insisted on listing slightly to the left. She stepped to the wall to adjust the painting for the third time.

Footsteps falling quickly along the steps leading down to the hall accompanied a cheerful whistle. Amy glanced over her shoulder to see who was coming.

"Frank." Her heart stopped, then started again, faster than before.

He stopped both feet and whistle in the middle of a musical phrase, staring at her. "Amy. I–I didn't know you were here. I had some business with Professor Headley and—" He waved a hand in a careless motion. "I guess you wouldn't care about that."

His words wounded her more deeply than any words since a boy in seventh grade had told her she was spindlier than his goat. The memory twisted amusement into the present pain. She didn't know how to respond to Frank's comment. Say "Of course I care; I care about everything that concerns you"? Such familiarity was beyond the bounds of propriety now that she was engaged to Walter.

Frank's gaze wandered from one picture to another. "Are these yours?"

"Yes." She slipped her hands into the pockets of the white apron protecting her dress. She didn't want him to see how she trembled at his nearness. Her fingers closed over the emerald ring she'd dropped into her pocket only minutes earlier. "Professor Headley kindly asked me to do a showing. He thought it would be nice for the students to see my work since I'll be teaching here this winter."

He walked along the wall, examining the paintings one by one. "I've only seen the paintings you did in school and some of your sketches. These are good. You've progressed a great deal in the last couple years." He shrugged. "Not that I'm an artist, but if it's obvious to me, it should be obvious to anyone."

His compliment was like balm to her aching heart.

Frank stopped in front of the picture of Pearl and straightened it. "This is your best, I think. I can feel the scorching summer wind that's blowing her hair and dress, and I almost smell the grain that's being harvested in the field she's looking out at."

"Thank you. Too bad you're not a buyer for the Metropolitan Museum."

"If you keep at it, maybe your work will hang there one day. After all, you won a state award last year, didn't you?"

She nodded, pleased he remembered.

"Are you going to keep it up after you're married?"

There it was, the marriage topic. "Of course. That is, I haven't thought. . .we haven't discussed it, but I can't imagine my life without painting."

"He won't mind if you teach?"

"He hasn't said so." She hadn't realized until this minute that such things might no longer be hers to decide. Marriage to Walter had meant only that she wouldn't be able to see Frank. The awareness that the marriage had further consequences staggered her.

"Maybe he'll take you to Paris to see the masterpieces there."

"You remembered." The words were out before she could catch them back.

Frank's eyes darkened, and it was as if he dropped a protective shield between them. "I remember your dream to study in Paris. I remember everything."

His gaze held hers captive. Her throat ached from repressed words, words that must never be spoken. *I remember everything, too, Frank. I always shall.*

His lips lifted in a small smile. "I remember when you came back from the Chicago World's Fair last year, all excited over Mary Cassatt's mural. You glowed when you spoke of her work."

"I'd love to meet her someday. There're so many questions I'd like to ask her. One can examine a master's paintings to see how the master obtained the results, but to actually have the opportunity to ask—"

"There you are, all excited again."

She dropped her gaze. Mary Cassatt's mural had depicted modern woman's liberation in education and professions, a contrast to a mural called "Primitive Woman," where the women were slaves to the men. Amy had never thought she'd marry a man who made her feel like a slave, but now. . .

"Why didn't you tell me, Amy?"

Her gaze jerked to his. The pain she saw cut through her. She knew, of course, what he meant: Why hadn't she told him she was going to marry Walter? "I intended to. I planned to tell you after the church service, but we went caroling, and there was Tom, then the open house at the parsonage, and then. . .then. . ."

"And then." He stepped closer, and it felt as though he gripped her shoulders and forced her to look into his eyes, though he didn't touch her at all. "Then you let me hold you." His voice was low but filled with indignation and betrayal. "You let me kiss you and believe we had chance at a future together."

Amy covered her face with her hands, unable to look on

his pain any longer. "I'm sorry."

"Did you know then? Did you know even then that you were going to marry Walter?"

She nodded.

"Do you remember you promised to allow me to court you, Amy? Do you remember when I offered to release you from that promise and you refused the release? Tell me, since your word has so little importance, do you plan to keep your wedding vows?"

His steps clipped angrily across the floor as he left. A sob ripped from her breast, and tears flowed into her palms.

❧

Frank stood in the barn doorway as light faded from the evening sky. He stuffed gloved hands into his jacket pockets and stared at the farmhouse. He didn't see the house surrounded by snow and insulating hay bales as it sat now. He saw Pearl gazing out to the harvest fields, waiting for Jason, as she stood immortalized in Amy's painting.

He remembered when Amy had started that painting, remembered coming in from the fields to find her sketching Pearl. Pearl had laughed, pleased and embarrassed all at once to be the subject of one of Amy's pictures.

He'd understood why Amy had selected Pearl and the theme, though Amy never explained it to him or anyone else in the family. The love between Pearl and Jason was living, vital. Jason wasn't in the picture at all, but a person knew from Pearl's expression that she was waiting for the man she loved and that the man she loved would come home to her.

All a man could wish for was represented in that picture.

During the last year he'd been glad for Jason that he'd found such a love with Pearl. He'd daydreamed that he and Amy would have a love that deep one day, after she'd traveled to Paris and he'd taken the agriculture course at the university.

Now seeing Jason and Pearl together only increased his

pain. They were a constant reminder of the future he'd lost with Amy. Maybe one day there'd be another woman for him.

Maybe, but he doubted it.

He shouldn't have let his temper get away from him at Windom Academy today. He'd replayed the questions he'd thrown at Amy one hundred times in his mind. He'd thought he'd feel better if he asked them.

He didn't. He didn't feel one whit better. Misery just kept growing in him like yeast in rising bread.

❧

Amy caught her bottom lip between her teeth and focused all her attention on trying to make the creamy sweep of paint bring her subject's cheek to life. She stepped back, palette in one hand, raised brush in the other, and studied the canvas with tilted head. Had she caught it, the way the light played over the cheekbone? "I think maybe I have at that, finally."

A clearing of a throat made her turn toward the door. "Yes, Lina?" She tried to keep the impatience from her voice. Sunlight was all too brief these winter days, but Lina didn't interrupt her in the studio often.

"Mrs. Sterling is here, Miss Amy. I know you aren't home to most visitors, but I thought you might be to her."

"You're right, Lina. Please show her up."

"Here? To the studio?"

"Yes." Amy laughed at Lina's surprise but understood it. She'd never accepted company in the studio before. But she had nothing to hide from Pearl.

She was still working on the portrait when Pearl entered. Glancing over at her guest, Amy said, "I'm so glad you came. Please, sit down. I hope you won't mind if I take advantage of a few more minutes of sunlight while we talk."

Pearl's practical black skirt swayed as she crossed the room. "Must I sit? I've never been in your studio before. What wonderful windows."

"I love this room. It's perfect for capturing the light. I hope Walter will build a similar room for me when we have our own home." She glanced up from her work. "Do the smells bother you? I confess, the oils and cleaning fluids are as welcoming to me as perfume."

"They don't bother me. May I see what you're painting?" Amy stood back so Pearl could see the entire canvas.

"Why, it's Frank."

"Then I've captured him. I mean, I've captured his image."

Surprise sat squarely in Pearl's blue eyes. "Yes, but why? I should think you'd choose to paint your betrothed, not a rejected suitor."

Amy's face heated. She'd been so involved in the painting that she'd forgotten for a few minutes that her subject was inappropriate. She hurried across the room and began cleaning her brushes.

Pearl remained beside the canvas. "Surely you aren't planning to hang this in the home you'll share with Walter. Did Frank commission it?"

"No."

"Amy, what is going on? We're best friends. I thought you were looking forward to courting Frank. You've always liked and admired him. You've told me so numerous times. Suddenly you're betrothed to Walter. I don't understand."

Amy poured water from a sprigged china pitcher into a matching bowl and rinsed her hands. "You're one to talk." She tried to keep her voice jolly. "You married Jason on the spur of the moment and right after another woman broke her engagement to him."

"That was different."

"Was it?" Amy laughed, truly amused. It felt good to laugh again. She couldn't remember laughing since Christmas Day.

"Amy Henderson, I've been in love with Jason since I was knee-high to a grasshopper, and you know it. You aren't in love with Walter. At least. . .you aren't, are you?"

"Why else do you think I'd marry him?" Amy busied herself with unfastening the cover-up she wore to protect her dress while painting. Pearl knew her too well. She'd easily read the truth in Amy's face.

Pearl spread her arms to her sides and dropped them. "I can't imagine."

"Walter is a good businessman. He'll be able to support a family well, even in these hard times."

"Do you love him?"

Amy hung her smock on a marble-topped hook beside the door. "People marry for reasons other than love all the time."

"I knew it! I knew you didn't love him."

"I didn't say that."

"You didn't say you do, either. And I've another question. Is Walter a Christian?"

The question had come to Amy's mind repeatedly. Each time she'd tried to ignore it as she now tried to ignore Pearl's challenging look and query. How could she admit she'd agreed to marry a man she didn't believe shared her faith?

Pearl clutched her stomach with one hand and with the other grabbed onto the easel beside her. "Oh, my."

Amy rushed to her, slipping an arm around her waist. "What is it? What's the matter? You're white as a sheet."

"I think perhaps your oils are too strong for me after all."

Amy hurried her out into the hall and shut the door behind them. "Sit in this window seat, and try to catch your breath." She lowered her friend to the flowered chintz cushions. "Don't move. I'll get a cold compress for you."

Pearl clutched Amy's wrist. "You'll do nothing of the kind. I'm fine."

"You're not fine."

"Yes, I am." She smiled, her blue eyes shining. "Jason and I are going to have a baby. We only found out a few days ago."

"A baby! I'm so glad for you." They shared an embrace. "But are you sure you're all right?"

"Yes, the paints made me nauseous is all. I'm feeling better already now that we're out of the studio."

Amy eyed her, dubious. "The color seems to be coming back to your cheeks."

Pearl patted the cushion beside her. "Sit."

Amy sat. "Yes, Ma'am."

"Don't think for a minute you're off the hook, as Jason would say. I want to know why you are marrying Walter."

Amy hesitated, watching her hands as she played with the folds in her gray wool skirt. It would be such a relief to share everything with someone. Pearl was her best friend. If there was anyone she could trust, it was Pearl. Besides, Pearl was like a sister to Frank. She'd understand how special he was, what grief Amy felt at losing him.

"You're right. I don't love Walter."

"I knew it." Pearl took Amy's hands. "Why are you marrying him?"

It tumbled out, the whole sordid story: her father's financial state, Walter's blackmail, her betrayal of Frank's trust. "That's the worst of it, that I've hurt Frank so. He has such a beautiful, compassionate heart, and I've treated him cruelly."

Pearl drew herself up, straightening her shoulders. "You can't do this, you know. You cannot marry Walter."

"Do you think I haven't racked my brain trying to find another solution? There isn't any other way out."

"There has to be. You can borrow the money."

"From whom? Using what for collateral?"

"I don't know much about business, but Jason and Frank should be able to figure something out."

"No!" Amy shot to her feet. "I told you everything in confidence because you are my dearest friend in all the world. You mustn't tell Frank and Jason. Promise me you won't."

Pearl stood, meeting Amy's gaze. "You should have exacted that promise before you told me. I won't be party to deceiving Frank, allowing him to believe you love Walter. Nor will I sit idly by and allow you to sacrifice yourself for your father."

Amy's hands closed into fists as she attempted to stop her trembling. "Pearl, please, you're my friend."

"That's why I won't make the promise you ask of me. Would you allow me to make such sacrifices? I'm going to tell Frank tonight, and you may as well get used to the idea."

Amy watched helplessly as Pearl swept down the stairs.

eleven

Amy looked over the edge of the walking bridge into the gully below, remembering the night her hat had sailed down among trees and bushes. Everything had still seemed possible and wonderful that night. The sweetness of walking home on Frank's strong arm wrapped around her in memory.

"Amy, wait."

She turned in surprise at Frank's call and watched him jog down the path from Windom. She hadn't seen him since Pearl had left her place the afternoon before. He must know the truth by now, all the terrible truths. She shuddered, dreading facing him, and dug her chin into the collar of her coat. Her glance darted over the institute grounds. There were no other students out, but that unusual condition wouldn't last long.

When he reached her, his gloved hands went immediately to her arms. "Pearl told me."

Amy cast her gaze to the ground. "I was afraid she would."

"Afraid?" Frank bent over until she had to look into his face. "Don't you know I wouldn't let Walter Bay harm you and your father this way?"

She gasped slightly. It was the gentleness in his tone and touch as much as his words that brought tears to her eyes. "There's nothing you can do. There's nothing anyone can do. But it means the world to me that you want to help us, that you care."

"Care? I'll say I care. We'll find a way out of this together. I promise we will." His eyes were lit with a tender fire.

Her lips wobbled when she tried to smile. "It's sweet of you to say that, but the only way you can help is to understand why

I am marrying Walter."

"Pearl said you don't love him. You don't, do you?"

"No, but it makes no difference."

"It makes all the difference. It's the only thing that makes any difference at all."

Students were beginning to come down the path. "Frank, you must leave."

"I'll walk you home. We can try to figure something out along the way."

Amy stepped back, pulling her arms gently from his hold. "Others are coming. I'm engaged to Walter. We can't be seen this way, and you mustn't walk me home."

"We're going to thrash this out, Amy." He didn't try to touch her again, but his tone left no doubt he meant what he said. "If you won't let me talk with you out here, I'll come to your home."

"No! Father might overhear, or Walter might show up."

"Then I'll send Pearl in to pick you up. You can come out to the farm with her. She'll be a perfect chaperon."

The other students were getting closer. Amy took another step back, shaking her head. "I don't think that's a very good idea."

"When do you want her to come? Tonight or tomorrow night?"

"Tonight, since you insist upon it." If she waited any longer, she'd chicken out for sure. "Good-bye." She turned about just as the other students reached the bridge.

❧

Amy arrived at the farm with Pearl and Jason, their spring wagon set on runners for winter. Frank came out of the house to greet them as soon as they drove into the farmyard. He helped Amy down from the wagon, his hands lingering on her waist a moment or two longer than necessary as he pressed his cheek against hers. For the first time since Walter had threatened her, Amy felt safe. She didn't believe Frank could do anything to help her, but she felt his love holding her up.

Once in the kitchen, Pearl took Amy's coat and hat. "You and Frank can talk in the parlor. We'll keep Frank's brothers and sisters out so you can have some privacy."

Amy looked from Pearl to Jason. "Don't forget, you've promised to take me home when I say I must leave."

Frank took hold of her elbow and directed her toward the parlor. "We aren't the ones kidnapping you, remember? Of course you're free to leave when you wish."

He pulled a high-backed spring rocker close to the parlor stove so Amy could warm up after the drive. Flames danced behind the stove's isinglass. The rose-colored globe on the hanging lamp spread soft, flattering light.

Frank drew an overstuffed green chair near the rocker and sat down. He leaned forward and took Amy's hands in both his own. "Thank you for coming."

"I only came because you threatened to come to my house if I didn't."

"I hope that's not true. I don't want to hurt you—I want to help."

"I understand that, but you can't help. It will only make things worse if you insist on trying."

"How could they possibly be worse?"

"Father could lose our home. His financial straits would become the talk of the town. It would destroy his pride." Amy heard her voice rise as she spoke.

"You're not alone in this anymore." Frank slid one of his hands slowly down her arm. The steady touch helped her catch the despair that had started spiraling out of control. "You didn't take Walter's word for it about your father's debt?"

"No." She told him about the mortgage papers Walter showed her and the ledgers and account books she'd found in her father's desk. "I feel so guilty, Frank. I should have realized Father might have financial problems."

One of her tears warmed the back of her hand. Frank passed his thumb tenderly beneath her eyes, catching more tears before they dropped. His kindness only increased her tendency toward weepiness.

"I've heard Father speak of the country's hard times at our very dinner table. Like everyone else, I know the Wall Street stocks almost collapsed in '93, that hundreds of banks and thousands of businesses have failed, even strong businesses like the railroads. Father always had a head for business and more than enough money for our needs. It never occurred to me he might lose everything, like so many others."

Frank's hands rubbed hers gently. "Shh. It's not your fault."

"But I've been so selfish. I bought new furniture for the dining room last spring, and he didn't mention economizing. I had a number of new winter outfits made. He said nothing, though he had not one thing made for himself. When I asked him why not, he said what he had was fine. I didn't question it, although it's not at all like him."

"He obviously wanted to protect you from the situation. I'm sure he believes he'll rebuild his financial base, that there's no reason for you to worry."

"He won't have a chance to rebuild if Walter calls his loan."

Frank lifted her hands, touched his lips to them, and cradled them against his cheek. "I love you, Amy. Marry me. We can live here on the farm, and your father will always have a home with us."

The sweetness of his love, the magnitude of his offer overwhelmed her. It wrapped around her like a chrysalis. For a moment she couldn't speak. This tender, protective love could be hers forever, but she had to turn it away. "I shall always treasure that you offered me this, me and Father. But I can't accept."

"Don't say that. Do you truly believe the money matters so much to your father that he'd want you to sell yourself into marriage?"

Amy cupped her hand about his cheek. "You can give Father a roof, but you can't save his pride. If Walter calls the loan and takes our house, everyone will know Father lost all his money. I don't know that his pride could bear that."

"Can his pride bear knowing you sold yourself for him?"

"He'll never find out."

"He will if I tell him."

Amy shot to her feet. "You wouldn't."

Frank stood, towering over her. "I'd do anything to keep you from marrying Walter. If you loved him, it would be different. Of course I wouldn't interfere then." His eyes widened. "You don't love him, do you? You said you didn't."

"I don't. How could you think I do after. . ." After the way they'd touched each other. "If you break my confidence by speaking with Father, I'll never forgive you. Even if your revelation meant I didn't marry Walter. If you tell Father, I'll never marry you, either." Amy started toward the kitchen.

He grabbed her arm. "Amy, please."

The anguish in his voice echoed the anguish in her soul. She steeled herself against it. "Thank you for your desire to help Father and me, but you will allow me to handle my own life." She stopped with her hand on the doorknob. She'd dreaded telling him this, but he must know it. "The wedding is planned for Saturday. Good-bye."

twelve

Remember Amy. Frank bolstered his courage as he headed down Main Street toward Walter Bay's office the next morning. *Jacob worked fourteen years for Rachel. Amy's worth at least that much to me.*

He adjusted himself to his horse's movements without an awareness of doing so, his mind on the task he'd given himself. He kept his gaze straight ahead when he passed Plummer's Saloon. Wished he'd never taken that first drink. Then he wouldn't be tempted to stop for one drink, only one, to give a nudge to his courage now.

You say You are all I need, Lord, and I sure need You now.

What he had in mind would save Amy's father's pride, if it worked, but it might destroy Frank's.

He tied his horse to the street-side railing, entered a wooden building, and headed up the steps to Walter's second-floor office. The pitch he planned to make went around in his head, as it had since he'd left home.

The odor of the cigars Walter liked filled the front room. The *clack-clack-clack* of a typewriter set a busy, modern note to the office. A young woman in a black skirt and white shirtwaist with a black bow at the collar looked up at him, and the clacking ceased. "May I help you?"

Frank pulled off his hat. "Yes, Miss. I'd like to talk with Mr. Bay."

"Who shall I tell him is calling?"

"Frank Sterling. I don't have an appointment."

The trim woman entered a door with Walter's name lettered on the frosted glass. Frank heard a murmur of voices through the closed door and transom. A moment later she held the door open for him. "Mr. Bay will see you now."

Walter didn't bother to stand or offer his hand when Frank entered. Instead the businessman leaned back and his oak chair creaked. "What can I do for you?" He stuck a cigar in his mouth and lit a match.

Frank didn't beat around the bush. "I understand you own the note on Mr. Henderson's house."

The match stopped halfway to the cigar. Walter shook it out. "That's right." He lit another match. This one made it to the end of the cigar. "How'd you hear about that?"

"I want to pay it off."

Walter leaned forward, elbows on his desk. "Excuse me?"

"You heard me. I want to pay off Henderson's loan."

A short laugh burst from Walter's mouth. "Do you have any idea how far behind Henderson is on that loan?"

"Yes."

"What are you planning to use to pay it off?"

Frank's grip on his hat tightened. "I can't pay it off all at once."

"Just the back payments?"

"I can't pay them off all at once, either." Frank kept his expression carefully solemn. He knew how ridiculous his offer sounded, but he only had a couple options.

Walter laughed again, relaxing against the chair back. "Maybe you should tell me what you have in mind that involves taking over the loan without making the payments."

Frank felt a flush rise up his neck and over his face. "I'll sign over my share of the proceeds from the sale of our crops."

"For this coming year?"

"For as many years as it takes."

Walter crossed his arms and looked Frank up and down.

Frank stood still, keeping his gaze steady.

"Why are you offering to do this?"

Frank didn't answer.

"You couldn't be this crazy about little Amy, could you?"

"Yes or no, Bay?"

"No, I think."

Frank's jaw tightened. He waited.

"Definitely no."

"I'll work for you. You can add my wages to my portion of the crops."

"Mm, mm, mm." Walter shook his head. "You want that little lady something fierce."

"What's your answer?"

"I'm not looking to hire anyone." He rolled his cigar between his thumb and forefinger. "There is one thing I'd consider."

A warning tingled along Frank's nerves. Nothing Bay came up with was likely to be honorable. "What's that?"

"I like a challenge as much as the next man. I hear tell you do, too. So how about a friendly little card game? All or nothing. You win, I sign over the note to you. I win, you sign over your share of the farm and I keep the note on the Henderson place."

Frank's heart picked up its beat. The forgotten but familiar excitement of the gambling dare raced through his blood. His conscience reminded him of the promise he'd made to God to give up gambling, but it looked like this was the only way to get rid of Henderson's debt and save Amy. Was his promise more important than that? "I'll have to think about it."

"Don't think too long. The offer's on the table until midnight. If you want to give it a toss, you'll find me above Plummer's Saloon."

≈

Frank couldn't keep his mind on classes at the Academy. All day he argued with himself and his conscience over Walter's challenge. Was the bet an answer to prayer?

I asked You to show me a way to help Amy and her father

out of this mess, Lord. I've tried everything that came to mind. This is the only way left. Does that mean I should take the challenge?

He'd heard too many sermons against gambling to trust it could be God's answer to his dilemma. Yet. . .

He'd offered Amy marriage, offered to take her father into their home, and she'd said no. It was important to her that her father's honor not be smirched.

He'd offered his income from the crops to Walter, offered to work for Walter, and those offers were also refused.

What else could he do? He'd spent sleepless nights wracking his brain for possibilities. He'd struck out on every idea. Wasn't it possible God's answer to his prayers was Walter's bet? If Frank won, and of course he'd win if this was God's plan, the debt would be wiped away and with it Walter's hold over Amy.

If I win, Amy won't need to marry Walter, but she won't marry me, either.

Amy and her father were as much against gambling as they were opposed to drinking. Frank hadn't forgotten his right to court Amy had been conditional on the promise he neither drank nor gambled for a year.

Mr. Henderson's cause for exacting that promise, Frank remembered all too vividly, was that Frank had been caught in a raid on what the newspaper called "the gambling den" above Plummer's Saloon, the very place Bay had set for the card game.

Frank's only consolation at the time had been that Ed Ray, another of Amy's suitors, had been caught in the same raid and consequently dropped from Amy's courters.

If I win the card game, I lose all chance at marrying Amy. If I don't take up Bay's challenge, I've lost Amy anyway.

❧

Frank's boots clunked against the narrow wooden stairs leading from the back of Plummer's Saloon up to the second floor. Laughter and loud conversation drifted up the stairwell. Smoke and the relaxing odor of drinks made from hops filled the air. The saloon was doing a brisk business, but that was normal for ten at night.

He stopped in the open doorway at the top of the stairs. He hadn't been in this room since the raid more than a year ago. He'd ended up in jail overnight and paid a fine, but the largest cost had been losing the opportunity to court Amy. Now he was back, hoping to win her freedom.

Still time to change my mind.

He pulled off his gloves, stuffed them into his coat pockets, and stepped over the threshold. The arguments hadn't stopped circling through his brain since he'd left Bay's office more than twelve hours earlier. He didn't like the choice he was making, but it was the only choice that gave him a chance to save Amy.

More tables filled the room than he remembered, probably brought from downstairs when the local law was enacted against tables in barrooms. A number of card games were going on, some with house dealers and some not. People lined a narrow table along one wall, calling encouragement to dice that danced with the people's dreams. In one corner a ball rattled as a wheel spun.

A rush of energy flooded him. He recognized it. That rush was the reason he'd enjoyed gambling.

Frank's gaze scanned the room for Walter and found him in the middle of a poker game. Frank made his way through the tables, returning greetings and turning down invitations to join in games. He stopped beside Walter's table as Walter pulled in a pile of winnings.

The irony of the situation wasn't lost on him. Mr. Henderson had tried to do right by Amy, demanding Frank not court her if he drank or gambled. She'd quit seeing Ed Ray after he had been caught gambling. Now, because of her father's debt, Amy might end up married to a man who made Frank and Ed look like amateurs in the world of drinking and gambling.

"Ah, you made it." Walter spoke around his cigar. "I was beginning to think you'd chickened out." He looked around at the others at the table. "You'll have to find a new game, boys. Next one is private between me and Sterling here."

"Hey, you need ta give us a chance ta win our money back," one of the players protested.

"Sure thing," Walter accommodated. "After the private game's over."

Frank took a seat across from Walter as one of the other players stood up. Most of the others hung around. Frank wished they'd move on but knew too well they wouldn't. A private game, no joiners allowed, might be high stakes. Could prove entertaining.

"Buy you a drink?" Walter asked.

"Sarsaparilla."

"Oo-oo-oo. Tough man."

The group about them guffawed. Frank smiled but didn't change his order. Not that it wasn't tempting. A drink would take the tension out of his shoulders. But even if he hadn't vowed to stop drinking, he didn't want alcohol crowding his thinking tonight.

Vowed not to gamble, too.

He pushed the thought away.

Walter called out to a young, mustached bartender who went downstairs to get the drinks.

"What's your pleasure?" Walter's eyes mocked Frank while he shuffled the cards.

"Your choice." His heart raced, but he tried to keep a calm demeanor. Nothing worse than a card player who couldn't keep a poker face. Easier to keep it if he started with it.

Walter announced his choice.

Frank gave one curt nod in agreement.

"What're the stakes?" the man who'd given Frank his chair asked loudly. "Gotta know the stakes before the hand's dealt."

Amy's happiness.

Walter pulled folded papers from his inside jacket pocket and tossed them on the table. Frank picked them up, unfolding them to scan them. The man behind his chair leaned close for a look. Frank pressed the papers to his chest. "This is private, George."

George stuffed his hands in his trouser pockets and took a step backward. "Private stakes in a public card game. Never heard of such."

The note appeared legitimate to Frank. He refolded the papers and laid them on the table, then pulled a note from his own coat and tossed it across to Walter.

Bay had no compunction with allowing others to see Frank's stakes. "Your share of the farm?" a man standing beside Walter burst out.

Heat flooded Frank's face, then receded so quickly he almost felt faint. If he went through with this game, the town was sure to find out about Henderson's financial troubles. George was right; high-stakes games didn't stay secret. Why hadn't he realized it before? Win or lose, he'd place Amy's father in the exact position she was trying so desperately to avoid.

But what else could he do? In less than a week Amy would be Walter's wife, and then nothing could change her fate. *There's no other way I can help her.*

thirteen

Is God limited to my help? The thought shouted in Frank's mind.

Walter's grin mocked him as he set the paper with Frank's signature down beside the Henderson note. "Nothing left to do but get started." He accordioned the deck between his hands.

"I want a new deck."

"Sure thing." Walter nodded at George. "Get us a new deck, would you?"

George hurried off. Walter and Frank stared at each other, Walter blowing smoke and grinning.

Frank tried to pray, but the question of whether he was limiting God kept getting in the way. Could he possibly trust God to help Amy, trust Him enough to walk away from this card game that appeared his only opportunity to save her?

His answer arrived at the same time George returned with the new deck of cards. Limited trust was no trust at all.

Frank pushed his chair back. "I've changed my mind."

Walter, new deck in his hands, stared openmouthed. "What?"

Frank reached for the note promising his share of the farm and stuck it in his pocket. Henderson's note remained on the table, looking innocent. Just pieces of paper, but the promises in them had the power to change lives.

Walter's laughter, loud and triumphant, stung Frank like whiplashes as he strode to the door.

❧

Amy's thoughts strayed again and again from the temperance-meeting speaker. The applause at the end of the speech startled her back to the church and the meeting. She joined belatedly in the clapping.

"Penny for your thoughts," Pearl whispered with a smile from the seat beside her.

"You wouldn't want them at any price." Self-pity wasn't worth the sharing.

The applause stopped as another speaker was introduced to the Women's Christian Temperance League. Amy listened to figures about alcohol that she could barely comprehend. More than a billion dollars was spent on alcohol every year in the United States, even during these hard times.

"How could that be?" the speaker asked. "How can people waste money on alcohol when there isn't enough to keep a roof over their family's heads?"

When the speech was over, Amy confided to Pearl, "I used to ask that same question in that same self-righteous tone."

"Which question?"

"'How can people waste money on alcohol when they can't afford to keep a roof over their family's heads?'"

Pearl frowned. "You don't ask that any longer? I do."

"I think Frank answered it for me, at least partly. He explained the people who drink heavily often do so to try to ease their pains and fears."

"The pains and fears are still there when they get done drinking."

"Yes." Amy didn't have the courage to say that for the first time in her life she could understand a person's desire to forget the painful places in life, even if for only a few hours. Not that she planned to resort to drinking herself, but in understanding that desire to escape, those who drank to excess had become more real to her. She realized in some ways she was just like them. If she hadn't been raised to believe Christ was sufficient in times of trouble and joy alike, would she have sought a way to forget her fears and responsibilities, even if it hurt the people she loved?

The WCTL president took the stage. "Before we adjourn in prayer, there are some questions I hope you will give serious consideration in the week ahead. Do you know any boys or young men who are beginning to drink? If so, have you pleaded and pleaded and pleaded with God for them? Have you felt as much real concern over them as you have over your winter coat or hat or a piece of furniture?"

She led them in a closing prayer, but her remarks left an impression on Amy's heart. Before Frank had laid his heart before her a year ago, she'd prayed for people to give up drinking but not with her heart and soul. Only because she cared so deeply for Frank had she learned to give depth to her prayers.

Was he tempted to go back to drinking because of the awful manner in which she'd treated him? If so, she was sure he'd fight the temptation, but she hated the pain she'd inflicted upon him. *Please, Lord, be with him. Lend him Your strength. Uphold him with Your everlasting wings.*

The meeting adjourned, and the women gathered about the refreshment table. Amy stayed in her seat, not eager to mingle. Beside her, Pearl rummaged through her reticule.

"Pearl, won't you change your mind and stand up for me at the wedding?"

"I should say not." There wasn't a second's hesitation in her answer. Pearl's hands stopped, and she grinned. "Unless you change your mind and your groom."

Amy didn't find her answer amusing. "I'd like you beside me. It would make it easier."

"Why should I make it easier for you to do something I think you shouldn't do at all?"

Mrs. Headley from the Academy and another woman stopped beside them. Amy thanked them for their excited congratulations on her upcoming wedding. She tried to appear happy and gracious. With dismay she realized they were only the first. It was the earliest opportunity for most of the women there to express their wishes, and Amy found herself surrounded.

When she was finally able to politely withdraw, she grasped Pearl's arm lightly. "Quick, let's get out of here before other well-wishers descend on me."

They collected their coats from the cloakroom. In the narthex, Pearl laid her hand on Amy's arm. "Has Walter told you that Frank spoke with him yesterday?"

"No." Dread made Amy's heart feel weighted. "What did Frank say?"

"Perhaps it's not my place to tell you, but I think you should know."

Amazement and gratitude flooded Amy when she heard Frank had offered the income from his crops and even offered to go to work for Walter. It humbled her to be loved that much. When Pearl told of Walter's offer to put Mr. Henderson's note up as stakes in a card game, Amy paled. She wasn't certain what was worse, the insult to her father or the fear that Frank had agreed to the game. "Did. . .did Frank?"

"Of course not," Pearl shot back.

Relief washed through her. "Good."

"Though he said he considered it. He only wants you and your father free of that man." Pearl pulled something from her purse and handed it to Amy. "Frank asked me to give this to you."

A wave of gratitude swept through her. She didn't know what was in the small brown book, but the fact that Frank wanted her to have it told her that he continued to forgive her for the pain she'd brought to him. She rubbed a hand lightly over the cover, admiring the gold cross and the words. *The Shadow of the Rock.*

"He sent a note with it," Pearl said. "I put it inside the

front cover. I need to be getting home. I hope I see you again before the wedding."

Pearl climbed up into the spring wagon and started down the street. Amy watched her friend and the wagon disappear, thinking about the incredible sacrifices Frank had offered to make for her. If it weren't for this painful place in their lives, if it weren't for Walter keeping them apart, she might never have known the depth of Frank's love.

Amy opened the book and removed a folded piece of paper:

> Dear Amy,
> Page 187.
> Always,
> Frank

She touched the word "always" with the tip of her index finger.

She flipped through the pages. The book was a collection of Christian readings, poetry, and the words to songs. She turned to page 187, curious. The reading on that page was titled "Hold On, Hold In, Hold Out." She read the first verse:

> Hold on, my heart, in thy believing!
> The steadfast only wins the crown.
> He who, when stormy waves are heaving,
> Parts with his anchor, shall go down;
> But he who Jesus holds through all,
> Shall stand, though heaven and earth shall fall.

"Oh, Frank," she whispered. Her eyes misted. The Lord must have known she needed this encouragement. How sweet that it came through Frank, that he understood she needed it. Whatever came, she would hold to Jesus and trust

Him to hold her up.

❧

Amy walked slowly along Windom Academy, fingers clasped lightly behind her back, looking at the pictures in her showing. Her students had viewed them earlier that day. It had given her a strange sensation to have her paintings viewed not only for enjoyment but also for instruction.

She shook her head. "My work isn't worthy, Lord," she spoke into the empty room. "I've so much to learn."

Would Walter allow her the opportunity? Perhaps by this time next year they would have a child, and her desires and commitments would be elsewhere.

"Your work is worthy."

Amy spun around at Frank's voice, her hand flying to her lace-enclosed neck. "I thought I was alone."

He leaned against an oak table set against the wall opposite the paintings. "Don't ever belittle your work. You might have more to learn—I expect that's true about everyone in every line of work—but you know more than most people in these parts. You offer the students here a lot."

"Thank you. I should remember to value the Lord's gift instead of judging it." She pressed her lips together hard and shook her head. "You were right about Walter's attitude. He told me he will allow me to continue teaching through the winter because the academy is counting on me, but after that he expects me to devote myself to. . .to being Mrs. Bay."

"I'm sorry."

She nodded. What else could either of them say about Walter's decision? "Thank you for the message, 'Hold on, my heart!' How did you know it was just what I needed?"

"I knew because it was just what I needed."

There were so many things she wanted to say and couldn't that her chest ached from the weight of them. "I wish things were different."

"You can change them."

Amy turned her back to him. "I can't. You know I can't. How can you attack me that way?"

His hands cupped her shoulders. "I didn't intend it as an attack." He turned her gently to face him. "I've been thinking lately a lot about the Bible story of Jacob and Rachel. Do you remember it?"

"Of course. Jacob loved Rachel and worked for her father for seven years for the right to marry her. Then her father deceived him. Jacob married Rachel's sister. He worked seven more years before Rachel's father allowed them to marry."

"Rachel's father manipulated Jacob and Rachel's lives and Rachel's sister's life, too. I wonder how they felt about his interference? I wonder if they resented it as much as I resent Walter running our lives."

"I resent it, too." Her words came out in a cracked whisper.

"I know."

He touched his lips to her temple. His arms slid around her shoulders, drawing her against his chest in a tender embrace.

Amy rested her head against him. She shouldn't allow his touch, but her heart belonged to him. He made her feel cherished. If God by some miracle gave her a way out of the marriage to Walter, she hoped to marry Frank. Whatever happened, of one thing she was certain: She loved Frank Sterling.

"During the last year when I was struggling to stay away from drinking, I held onto your trust in me to help get through."

Shame washed over her. "And in the end I wasn't able to keep my promise that we'd court."

"I'm not accusing you. I'm trying to apologize, to tell you I was wrong. I made my promise to stop drinking when I told Christ I wanted to follow Him and His ways. I was wrong to tie that promise to you." His hands framed her face, and she trembled as he looked deep into her eyes. "I could only stop drinking for myself, with Christ's help, not for you. That's what I've learned since you became engaged to Walter."

Her smile was shaky. " 'He who Jesus holds.' "

"Yes." Frank took her hands in his. "I thought you were perfect, Amy, but you're not. Only Christ is perfect. Remember how Rachel's father manipulated Rachel's life?"

She nodded.

"With the very highest intentions, you're manipulating your father's life."

Amy tore her hands from his. Anger and hurt made it seem her heart pounded in her ears.

"I'm sorry, Amy, but it's true." Frank reached to recapture her hands.

She stepped back, placing her hands behind her. "Don't touch me."

"Listen, please. I know you're trying to save your father from embarrassment, to save him from losing his house. But you aren't trusting him to be man enough to face his own responsibilities. How do you think your father will feel when he learns about your sacrifice after you're married and he can't change what you've done?"

"He won't find out."

"Do you honestly trust Walter not to tell him?"

She saw the pity in his eyes and hated it. He was right, of course. Walter wasn't trustworthy. But what could she do other than hope this one time would be different?

"How will your father feel when he discovers you haven't let him decide how to handle his own debt or decide what sacrifices he's willing to make for himself? Your loving intention is to give your father a gift by marrying Walter, but you're taking away your father's right to run his own life, the way Rachel's father took that right away from his daughters and Jacob, and the way Walter is trying to take it away from us."

"No! You're willfully misinterpreting everything." Tears

streamed down her face, but she was past caring. "You don't care about my father. You only care about yourself. You'll say anything—all these awful things—to stop me from marrying Walter."

"Amy, you couldn't save me from drinking, and you can't save your father from his problems. It may seem you can for awhile, but in the end, each person, with God's help, has to rescue himself, even your father."

"Go away." She buried her face in her hands. "Please, go away."

She could barely hear his footsteps leaving over the sound of her sobs.

fourteen

Frank rushed through the front door of Windom Academy and down the stone steps, blind to the snow-covered prairie before him. He'd known he was risking her anger in trying to make her see things from her father's perspective, but that didn't stop it from hurting. Would she forgive him one day, or would she allow this to fester into hatred? If she married Walter, it might be easier for her if she didn't love another man. Still, already the estrangement between their hearts left his soul scorched.

The winter wind whipped hard little snowflakes into his face. He pulled up his jacket collar and wrapped his muffler around his neck against nature's fury as he headed toward the shed where the horses were kept.

A drink would take the edge off the wind's chill—and the chill of Amy's anger.

He pushed the thought away. Would he always face that temptation? If only he could be done with it once and for all. He had no intention of drinking again, but the thought did creep in every time he faced something hard.

The smells of straw and horses were welcoming in the dark shed. He lit a kerosene lantern that hung beside the door. His boots crunched in the straw as he crossed the shed to saddle his horse.

The shed door creaked open, letting in a shaft of sunlight and gust of wind and snow, then creaked shut. "Frank Sterling, you in here?"

"Over here, Professor Headley, by the lamp." Frank settled a saddle blanket over his horse's back. "Come spring, we need to build a decent stable," he said, only half joking.

The professor sighed. "We could barely afford this shed, even with the students doing the labor. Money is tight."

Frank grunted as he lifted his saddle from the straw. "That it is. Tight everywhere." *So tight it's strangling the life from Amy and her father.*

Professor Headley leaned against the post on which the lamp hung, his hands stuffed in his coat pockets. The light cast shadows over the slender man's angular face beneath his derby.

"Frank, there are some questions I need to ask that I'd rather not. I meant to ask you to come to my office to talk, but I didn't catch you before you left the building."

Surprise mixed with trepidation sent a warning through Frank's chest. Had the professor overheard him and Amy? Was he going to accuse Frank of besmirching Amy's honor? What else could the professor possibly question that would be a delicate topic? Frank had to swallow twice before he could speak. "Ask away, Professor."

"You know the Academy allows no leniency if a student is caught drinking or gambling."

Frank's hands froze on the saddle belt he'd just cinched. "Yes, Sir."

"Someone reported to me this afternoon that you'd been seen coming out of Plummer's Saloon a few nights ago." Professor Headley's voice sounded almost apologetic.

"You're asking whether it's true."

"Yes."

"It's true I was in the saloon."

"I see."

The disappointment in the kind man's voice cut into Frank's chest. "I didn't drink any liquor, and I didn't gamble, though I admit I came close on both counts. I'm not proud of that."

"I'm glad to hear you only came close. Unfortunately, the

school rules say you will be suspended from classes until this matter is resolved."

The pain in Frank's chest grew. "How do I go about clearing myself of the charges?"

"You'll need to find someone to confirm your statement that you didn't drink or gamble while inside the saloon. Then it will be up to the directors to decide whether they believe you and your witness."

Witness. Sounded like a court of law. Might as well be for the sentence they could impose on him. "I'm sure I can find someone to stand up for me."

"Be aware that the word of anyone who was in the saloon with you might be considered suspect by the directors."

He hadn't thought of that, but it made sense. "Thank you for the warning. Is there anything else, Sir?"

"The man who brought the accusations to me is one of the directors."

"Am I allowed to know who it was?"

"Walter Bay."

Hope plummeted. *I should have known.* It was like Walter to do this. He'd have a good laugh over it, knowing Frank would never tell that he'd been at the saloon to meet Walter, never reveal Amy's secret by telling of Walter's challenge.

"Is there anything else, Sir?"

"No. Except. . .I'm sorry, Frank."

Frank nodded. "Good day, Sir." Numbness set in as he led his horse from the shed into the sharp sunlight. How much more could go wrong in his life?

&

Amy slumped against the wall across from her paintings. Her handkerchief was sodden, she had a headache, and her stomach muscles hurt from crying, but still the tears came. Frank's arms had provided a refuge, albeit a bittersweet one. Then his words turned everything into bitterness. How could he have been so cruel? Didn't he understand how difficult it was for her to marry Walter? It was so important to her that Frank understood.

"Amy?"

At Mrs. Headley's voice, shame and consternation increased the weariness in the wake of Amy's sobbing.

The professor's wife slipped her arms around Amy's shaking shoulders. "My dear, what is it? Nothing's happened to Walter, has it?"

Amy could only shake her head. Words wouldn't come through her sob-filled throat.

"There, there. Cry it out, whatever it is." Mrs. Headley patted Amy on the back gently.

"I don't know wh–what's g–gotten into me," Amy said in a sob–stutter when she could finally speak. "I n–never c–cry." Of course, she knew exactly what had caused the crying spell, but she couldn't possibly admit she was crying because she loved one man and was marrying another.

Mrs. Headley handed her a clean handkerchief. "Wedding jitters. Every bride is entitled to at least one good cry."

Amy looked curiously at the headmistress. Mrs. Headley wasn't much older than she. "I can't imagine you crying before your wedding. You and the professor are so dedicated to each other."

"I admit I've never been happier. But marriage changes a woman's life forever. It's a sensible woman who questions whether she is doing the right thing when she marries."

"It's a joy to see the way you and your husband work together for the academy."

"We love the academy. It's exciting to see it grow, but some aspects are difficult."

Amy dabbed at a lingering tear. "I know the funds have been difficult to raise."

"That isn't the worst of it." Mrs. Headley sighed. "One of

our students was seen frequenting a saloon. It's always sad when we have to ask one of our young men to leave the school, but we must guard the morals of the other students."

Amy nodded.

"I'm especially disappointed this time," Mrs. Headley continued. "My husband and I try not to play favorites, but just between you and me, we did especially like Mr. Sterling."

"Frank?" Shock jolted the last of the sobs from her lungs.

"Yes. Such a polite, intelligent young man."

Amy grasped Mrs. Headley's arms. "When was he accused of being at the saloon? Was it Plummer's Saloon?"

Mrs. Headley gasped. Her eyes widened.

Amy dropped her hold, mortified at her behavior. "I'm sorry. I didn't mean to grab you that way. It's just that it's so important. When was Frank accused of being at the saloon?"

"I'm not certain. It was within the last few days."

"Oh, no." Had Frank known of the accusations when he and she argued, Amy wondered? It would be so like him to spare her the knowledge. If he were dismissed from the Academy, it would be for attempting to help her. She should be devoted to Walter, yet everything she learned about Frank, everything he did, increased her admiration and love for him.

"Amy, what can you possibly know about this?" Mrs. Headley's words held not only curiosity but a hint of disapproval.

Amy's thoughts raced. If she told what she knew, she'd expose to Professor Headley the very things she'd tried so hard to keep private. If she saved her own reputation and her father's, Frank might be expelled. Attending the academy was so important to him.

She took a deep breath. "I think I'd better speak with your husband."

The professor wasn't in his office or in the rooms in Windom Academy that he and his wife shared. Mrs. Headley and Amy finally learned the professor had gone to get some supplies at the general store. Mrs. Headley invited Amy to join her and the students who roomed at the Academy for dinner, but Amy declined. She was glad when Mrs. Headley went to oversee dinner, leaving Amy to relax in the room that served as the Headleys' parlor.

A simple kerosene lamp on a small parlor table was lit against the early winter evening darkness. Amy paced the small, sparsely furnished room, praying. "Hold on, my heart," she encouraged her soul.

Professor and Mrs. Headley entered the parlor following dinner. Almost immediately Mrs. Headley left the room on the pretense of hanging up his outer coat and derby. Amy was grateful for the woman's courtesy in offering them privacy. The professor invited her to sit in an oak rocker, and he sat across from her in a stiff-backed chair. "My wife tells me you believe you have knowledge concerning Mr. Sterling's frequenting of Plummer's Saloon. I find this difficult to believe, but I'm willing to listen."

"You will keep this in confidence, Sir?"

"As much as I am able. The situation will be brought before the directors, of course. If what you say truly relates to Mr. Sterling's guilt or innocence, it may be necessary to share it with the directors."

Amy caught her bottom lip between her teeth. She'd convinced herself of the need to expose her situation to Professor Headley, but to the directors? Secrets didn't remain secrets once one began sharing them. Little by little they leaked out into the community. *But if I don't tell, Frank will be suspended.*

She took a deep breath, lifted her chin, and looked the professor squarely in the eyes. "I believe you will understand the need for discretion when you hear my story. Mr. Sterling was at the saloon because of me."

A log broke and crashed in the fireplace. The flames cast strange shadows across the professor's face.

"Miss Henderson, are you aware of what you're saying?"

She flushed but kept her gaze steady. "Perfectly." She explained succinctly about her father's inability to pay his mortgage and Walter's offer to Frank to put the note up for stakes in a card game. She left out that her engagement to Walter was a result of blackmail.

The professor rested his elbows on the arms of the chair and pyramided his fingers. "Do you know whether Mr. Sterling participated in this card game?"

"No, he did not."

"How do you know this?"

"His sister-in-law told me."

"If Sterling was intent on saving your father's honor, why did he change his mind?"

"I can't answer for him, Sir."

A knock at the door made her jump. The professor answered the door and ushered in three guests: Frank, Jason, and a young man who looked vaguely familiar but whom she couldn't place.

Shock at the sight of her filled Frank's eyes.

A tremble rippled along her nerves. Earlier Frank had accused her of interfering in her father's life. Would Frank hate her now for interfering in his own life?

fifteen

Frank stopped short. "Amy. I mean. . .Miss Henderson, I didn't expect to see you here." He whipped his hat off.

Jason and the other young man followed suit.

Frank eyed Amy nervously. He'd never imagined he would see her here the night before her wedding.

"What can I do for you young men?" Professor Headley asked.

"We're here about that incident we discussed earlier." Frank hoped the professor realized the need for discretion. "I didn't know you had company. We can come back another time."

"You may have arrived right on schedule." The professor nodded at Amy. "Miss Henderson believes she has knowledge that may help your case."

Frank felt the blood drain from his face. "I don't think that's possible, Sir."

"It seems unlikely to me, too," Headley agreed, "yet she wishes to speak on your behalf. Perhaps you have something to say which will make her contribution unnecessary?"

"I hope so." He glanced at Amy. Her cheeks were rosier than he'd ever seen them indoors. Anguish filled the eyes that looked back at him. He turned to the professor. "You've met my brother, Jason. I asked him to accompany me when I went to find a witness to my actions at the saloon. I didn't want to be accused a second time of drinking while I was there." He nodded toward the other man. "This is Mr. Peters, a bartender at Plummer's. Mr. Peters, this is Professor Headley."

The men shook hands.

"I assume Mr. Peters is here to shed light on your activities?" Headley asked.

"Yes."

Headley turned to Peters. "And what do you have to say, Sir?"

"Frank here, he came into the saloon, all right, but all he ordered was a sarsaparilla."

"Are you certain?" Headley questioned. "Isn't it hard to remember what one person ordered?"

Peters grinned. "Not when it's sarsaparilla. Not many men come to a saloon for a tame drink like that."

"Were you the only bartender that night?"

Peters hesitated. "I was the only bartender in the room Frank here was in."

"I understand Mr. Sterling was invited to join a card game at the saloon."

Peters's gaze shifted to Frank, then the floor, then back to the professor. "Card games and gambling ain't allowed in Chippewa City."

Frank recognized the apprehension in Peters's eyes and understood it. Frank wasn't allowed to drink or gamble if he wanted to remain enrolled at the Academy, but there was no law against selling liquor in the saloon. There was, however, a law against gambling. Peters didn't mind verifying the sarsaparilla, but he wouldn't threaten his job by admitting to the gambling. Where had Headley heard about the game? Surely not from Amy.

Peters stepped toward the door, worrying his hat brim. "Uh, I need to be getting back to work."

Headley held the door for him. "Thank you for coming."

"Yes, thanks," Frank added.

Jason offered to take Peters back to the saloon and then return for Frank. "I expect you and the professor need to have a few more words."

Headley closed the door behind Jason and Peters, then leaned back against it, arms crossed over his chest. "It appears there's a lot more here than meets the eye, Mr. Sterling. Miss Henderson tells me Mr. Bay asked you to join him in a card game with a note for stakes, a note on her father's house. She says you backed out of the game. That seems strange, since evidently you went to the saloon for the sole purpose of participating in that game."

How much had Amy told him? Frank didn't want to reveal more of Amy's situation than she had already done. "I wanted to get that note out of Mr. Bay's hands, Sir. I don't trust the man and don't like to see Mr. Henderson in debt to him. But I made a promise to give up gambling over a year ago. In the end, I couldn't go through with the game. Just didn't seem good could come from breaking my vow that way."

Headley rubbed a hand over his beard. "If we bring this situation before the directors, it's certain there will be questions that no one involved with the gambling at Plummer's will be willing to answer honestly. I know there's something you two aren't telling me, but I'm going to accept your word, because I can't imagine why Miss Henderson would lie for you about this, Mr. Sterling."

Relief poured through Frank, both for himself and for Amy. "Thank you, Sir."

"Thank you," Amy echoed.

Headley pursed his lips. "Mr. Bay isn't a student at the Academy, but he is a director. I don't like the idea of allowing a director to get by with behavior that results in expulsion for a student. Yet I can't expect you to speak against your betrothed, Miss Henderson."

"No, I couldn't do that." Her voice was soft.

"And you, Mr. Sterling?"

"I think not."

"No, I didn't think so." Professor Headley shook his head slowly. "I don't know for certain what's happening here, but I have my suspicions. Yes sir, I definitely have my suspicions, and they aren't pleasant. I suggest you two spend some time searching your hearts—alone—and a lot of time on your knees."

Frank accompanied Amy to the front door of the Academy, where they waited for Mrs. Headley to join them. When Jason returned, they would take Amy home, with Mrs. Headley chaperoning. It would take a bit of time going back and forth, but with Amy marrying Walter in twenty-four hours, her reputation needed to be protected more than ever.

"I'll never forgive myself for putting you in this position," Frank told her, "and never stop thanking God that you cared enough to speak up for me to Professor Headley."

Amy leaned against the door, watching out the window. "I didn't tell him Walter is blackmailing me into marrying him. I hadn't that much courage."

"I'm glad you didn't." The words came out more fervently than he'd intended. He cleared his throat. "I wish. . .I wish you loved Walter."

She swung around, and surprise sat large in her eyes.

"I mean it. Since you're determined to marry him, I wish you were crazy in love with him. I want you to be happy every moment of your life."

Her face gentled into a smile so sweet he thought he could hang the stars on it. "I want the same for you, Frank."

He ached to hold her and never let her go. At least it brought some comfort to know she understood he loved her, and she loved him.

Mrs. Headley's footsteps clipped along the hallway on her way to join Frank and Amy.

Frank allowed his gaze to tell Amy one last time that he loved her, but all he said was, "Hold on, Amy. Hold on."

sixteen

Amy sat in front of her walnut vanity, watching the mother-of-pearl-backed handle move back and forth in smooth strokes as she buffed her nails. The grandfather clock in the first-floor hallway sounded dimly in her room. Five strikes. Two hours until the wedding. In a little over two hours in the parlor downstairs she'd become Mrs. Walter Bay.

The trunk beside the tall walnut shrank was filled with her clothes. Only the suit she planned to wear after the wedding remained in the shrank. A few things still covered her vanity: the brush, comb, and buttonhook that matched her nail buffer; the jewelry she planned to wear with her gown; the little brown book from Frank with its brave gold cross on the front; the miniature skaters in their glass dome.

She wished she and Frank had a dome to protect themselves from the pain of the years to come.

A quiet knock at her door brought her from her reverie. "Come in."

Pearl stuck her head inside the door. "Am I still welcome?"

"Of course." Amy set the buffer carelessly beside the matching vanity accessories and stood, meeting Pearl with a hug in the middle of the room. "What are you doing here?" A terrible thought filled her with dread. "Is Frank all right?"

"He's fine physically. Wallowing in misery, of course." Pearl took a deep breath. "I know I told you I wouldn't stand up for you at your wedding, but I've changed my mind, if you'll have me."

Amy threw her arms around her friend again, joy and relief flooding her. "I'd love to have you."

"If you asked someone else, I'll gladly take my place as a simple guest."

"No, I've asked no one else. You and Jason are the only friends I asked to the wedding. Father asked a couple friends, as did Walter. Walter hasn't any family here. Lina and Mrs. Jorgenson are helping with the guests. I thought if I must have someone stand up for me, I would ask one of them at the last minute. I didn't want anyone but you. I'm so glad you changed your mind."

Pearl sat on the edge of the brocade-covered bedstead and sighed. "I'm embarrassed to say it took Frank to bring me to my senses. He reminded me we need to honor others' decisions, even when we don't agree with those decisions. He said, 'God gives us free will. We should honor each other as much as God honors us and not try to force our will on others.' " She raised her chin in a defiant manner. "I may not believe marrying Walter will make you happy or that it's a good answer to your problems, but you have the right to marry whomever you choose, and I'll love you even when you're Walter's wife." She wrinkled her nose. "I may need to continue thinking of you as my friend Amy instead of Mrs. Walter Bay to keep my good intentions, though."

A laugh bubbled up from Amy's chest, and she dropped down on the bed beside Pearl. "Thank you. I thought I'd lost everyone important in my life except Father." Amy hadn't the slightest doubt that Pearl's presence was a gift from both their heavenly Father and Frank, and as such, Pearl was doubly, triply welcome.

Pearl laid her hand on the small bulge at her middle. "Is it in poor taste to stand up for you in my condition?"

"It's always perfect etiquette to act in love for another, isn't it? It must be wonderful to be expecting a child with the man you love." Frank would make a doting father and a doting husband to the mother-to-be. Sadness at what might have been dampened the spirits Pearl's arrival had lifted. Amy refocused her thoughts with determination. She'd chosen to marry Walter, whatever the reason. No use remaining a weeping Wilma about it. "Besides, you aren't large enough yet for anyone to more than suspect you're expecting a baby."

Pearl ran a hand along her turquoise silk skirt. "I wore my best gown for your wedding. It's last year's Christmas gown, altered for my condition, of course. I've let out a number of outfits already. Soon I'll need to give in and make something more appropriate from scratch, though it seems such an extravagance in these hard times."

There it is again, Amy thought, *the awareness of the need to economize. Am I the only person who went along blissfully unaware of the Panic's effect on daily life? I've thought only of myself. No wonder Father and I are in this unsavory situation.*

Joy shone forth from beneath Pearl's comments regarding the necessary work and economy in accommodating her growing size. Amy envied her. Raising children with Frank would have been wondrous fun. He'd make a marvelous father. She shuddered to think what kind of father her possible children had to look forward to in Walter.

Pearl straightened her back. "Here I am going on about myself when we need to get you ready for your wedding. Your gown is exquisite!" She moved quickly across the room to the shrank, where an ivory satin gown hung.

Amy followed slowly. "I tried to convince Father that one of my other new winter gowns would do as well, but he insisted I have the latest thing. I couldn't think of a way to argue him out of it without revealing my knowledge of his financial affairs." She fingered the puffed shoulders above narrow lace sleeves. "I'd hoped the dressmaker would solve the situation for me by insisting she couldn't make the gown so quickly. I'm afraid she worked night and day to complete it."

"And completed it beautifully." Pearl pulled the gown out

from the shrank to view the back. "Oh, my. We'd best begin dressing you now. It will take hours to fasten all the satin-covered buttons on the back and sleeves."

Everything inside Amy withdrew, revolting against donning the gown that represented the demise of Amy Henderson and the birth of Mrs. Walter Bay. She removed her wrapper and laid it over the end of the bed, wishing desperately that time would stop moving.

It seemed hours later that Pearl fastened the last button.

"Finally." Amy heaved a sigh. "My feet are giving out."

"Don't sit down. You'll wrinkle your gown."

"Wish I'd thought of that before putting it on. I still haven't done my hair."

Pearl glanced about. "I can stand on the vanity bench while I work on it." They laughed at the sight they made while she piled Amy's thick, soft brown hair in a bouffant topknot. She tucked orange blossoms around the knot. "Beautiful. Do you have a veil?"

"No."

"Jewelry?"

Amy put on a pair of simple drop pearl earrings. Then she took from the vanity drawer a gold bow pin with a delicate oval, etched gold locket attached, and pinned it to the left breast of her gown. *Above my heart,* she thought.

She met Pearl's glance in the mirror. A frown crinkled her friend's brow. "Um, I don't think that's the usual jewelry to wear with your bridal gown."

Amy ran her fingertips lightly over the cool gold. Not even with Pearl would she share the full truth about the locket. The front opened to reveal a timepiece. The back held a secret opening. Inside was a picture of her mother on one side. The other held a miniature painting she'd made of Frank. She told Pearl a partial truth. "The locket belonged to my mother."

The frown cleared. "Then of course you must wear it. I

wish I'd had something of my mother's to wear at my wedding." Pearl laid a gentle hand on Amy's shoulder.

Amy covered Pearl's hand with her own, a pang of empathy touching her heart. "Weddings seem meant to be shared with mothers, don't they?"

Their gazes met again in the mirror. Pearl dashed away a tear from her lashes and smiled. "What's next?" Her tone obviously meant to break the emotional moment.

Amy hesitated. "Do you remember the painting you saw me making of Frank?"

Pearl nodded.

"I can't keep it. There's no telling what Walter might do if he saw it. I can hardly leave it here in the house. Father would wonder if he came across it. Will you take it home, please?"

"You know I will." Pearl rearranged a curl in front of Amy's ear. "If you don't mind my saying so, I think that's wise. Anyone who saw it would know immediately that you care deeply for him."

Amy's heart tripped. She hadn't realized she'd exposed her love for Frank to the world in that picture. As an artist it was a compliment. As a woman marrying another man, well. . . . "It's in the shrank, wrapped in a soft cloth. I'd like Frank to have it. I suppose it's inappropriate to give it to him, but then," she shrugged and gave a sharp little laugh that rose from her shattered heart, "it seems everything about my life is inappropriate."

"They say time heals all things," Pearl said softly.

"They?"

"People who've lived a lot longer than you and me."

People who hadn't loved Frank Sterling and married Walter Bay. What did they know? She took a deep breath. " 'He who Jesus holds through all, shall stand, though heaven and earth shall fall.' "

"Yes, thank God. Um. . .I think you've forgotten something, Amy."

Amy raised her eyebrows in question.

"Your ring."

Amy removed the emerald ring from the drawer and slid it on her finger. It felt like the weight of the world.

There was a loud knock at the bedroom door.

"Come in, Lina," Amy called.

The door opened. "It's not Lina. It's the proud papa coming to see his daughter one last time before giving her away."

Tears distorted Amy's image of her father's round smiling face above his formal black cutaway coat and white shirt and vest. The words "giving her away" struck her as especially and awfully true. She didn't want to be given away. She didn't want to go away at all.

"Amy's a lovely bride," Pearl assured him. "I'll give you two a few minutes alone. I'll be down the hall on the window seat if you need me." She closed the door behind her.

"Let me look at you." Mr. Henderson's voice was softly gruff, and Amy knew he was having difficulty keeping a check on his emotions.

She turned around slowly. When she stopped, she saw his eyes had reddened.

"Mrs. Sterling is right; you are a lovely bride. The loveliest ever, except for your dear mother." He reached for Amy's hands. "I do wish your mother could be here today. I don't know that I've ever told you, but she'd be busting her corset stays in pride over the woman you've become."

"Father!" She giggled at his unusual language. She suspected he used it to add levity to the situation.

"I hope Walter will bring as much happiness to your life as your mother did to mine." He glanced about the room with its embossed floral wallpaper and pale blue window hangings. "Remember how many hours you and your mother spent planning this room? Nothing would do but that you had the exact shade of blue you wished in the hangings and that your bed be the finest your mother could find."

"I do remember." Amy smiled at the heart-warming remembrance.

"Some of my fondest memories lie in planning and furnishing this house with your mother." He lifted his big round shoulders in a self-conscious shrug. "More to the truth, she and I planned it, and she did the furnishing." His gaze swept the room, and he sighed. "It's a mighty big house for a man to ramble around in alone. Maybe I should think of selling it."

Amy's heart faltered. "S-sell it? Mother's house?"

"She did love it, but she has a better one now."

"But. . .but the memories. Could you bear to leave them behind?"

He shook his head, smiling down at her. "Oh, Sweetheart, don't you know we never leave the memories behind? They live in our hearts."

Confusion turned her mind to balls of cotton. She'd thought it would all but kill her father to lose this house, but now he spoke of selling it. Frank's accusation from the day before leaped into her thoughts: "You're taking away your father's right to run his own life."

Pearl had just commented on honoring others' rights to make their own decisions. Honoring. The word used in the command, "Honor your mother and father." Was not trying to save them from their problems without allowing them a chance to decide whether they wanted the help a form of honoring them? Frank and Pearl were honoring Amy's decision. *Would I want my father making sacrifices for me without giving me the chance to make my own sacrifices, my own decisions?* The answer flashed sure and swift in her soul. *No, I wouldn't want Father to lie to me, even to save me from something awful.*

"Why the frown?" Her father lifted her chin. "A bride should wear a smile, and a radiant one at that."

Amy took a deep breath. "I think we need to talk."

"Now? It's almost time for the wedding to begin. There'll be plenty of time to talk afterward." He chuckled, his stomach stretching the coat buttoned across it. "It's not as though Walter's carrying you across the continent to live. His house is only a few blocks from here."

Amy laced her fingers together in front of her. "I'm sorry to keep the guests waiting, but what I have to say needs to be said now or not at all."

"Sounds ominous." His voice was light, but she could see the concern in his eyes. Worry for her, no doubt.

"I'm afraid I've acted high-handedly and pridefully."

His brow furrowed in confusion. "About what?"

"You."

"Me?"

Amy nodded, catching her bottom lip between her teeth. She searched for a way to begin. "I've tried to solve a problem for you without letting you decide whether you want me to solve it."

His round cheeks shook with his chuckle. Relief danced with the amusement in his eyes. "I thank you for wishing to help me, but I can't imagine any problem of mine which you could solve, especially behind my back."

"I thought the same thing a couple of weeks ago."

"What happened then to make you so wise?" A remnant of his chuckle reverberated in his chest.

She dropped her gaze to the floor, unable to meet his eyes. Sorrow over the pain she knew her revelation would cause her father made her throat feel swollen and sore. It took an effort to speak, and the words came out a whisper. "I found out you're behind on the mortgage on this house and have lost most of your money."

A moving shadow brought her gaze up. Her father had grabbed the bedpost with one hand. His face was ashen.

Amy gasped and reached for him. "Father!"

seventeen

Mr. Henderson waved his free hand and shook his head. "I'm all right."

His words didn't reassure Amy. He looked ill. Why, oh why, hadn't she left well enough alone?

He sat down heavily on the bed. "How did you find out? When?"

"A week before Christmas. Walter told me."

"Walter?" Disbelief filled his still-whitened face. "I suppose he thought you had a right to know since you're going to be his wife." He shook his head slowly. "I wanted to spare you the worry of it all. Everyone is living on credit these days. My business contacts have been understanding in extending me time. I hoped I could get by until you married. I don't mind so much for myself losing my money, but for you. . . ."

A small cry escaped her. She dropped to her knees, heedless of her dress, and grasped his hands. "I don't care about the money for myself. My concern is for you. I didn't want you to be embarrassed in front of your friends and business associates."

"Most of my business associates already know I've lost money in my investments and can't pay my bills. It's a little embarrassing, yes, mainly because I've believed an honorable man pays his debts. But everyone is having money trouble since the Panic. I hope if I hang on long enough, I'll eventually be able to pay those who have trusted me by extending me credit."

"What if the people you owe demand the money? Can't they force you to. . .to sell the house, for instance, to raise money?"

"Yes, and if they demand their money, then it's only right I sell the house or anything else I can to raise it. Of course, in the present economic situation there aren't many who can afford this place, even at the reduced price the times demand." He frowned. "Just how did you plan to solve my money problems? Did you sell a painting for a stupendous price and forget to tell me about it?"

"I wish." She laughed in spite of her heavy heart. She was glad to see color returning to his face. "My plan won't solve all your money problems. Only one."

"I'm still mystified. Which one?"

"The mortgage."

His thick white brows met in confusion. "Walter hasn't demanded payment on the note."

"Not from you."

"Who else would he demand it from?"

Amy saw the truth begin to dawn in his eyes.

"He asked you to pay it? His own betrothed?" Shock and scorn saturated his words.

"After a fashion. He, um, said he would demand immediate payment in full if I didn't marry him, and—"

"What?" He shot to his feet. His lips trembled in anger. "He dared demand that of you?"

She rose hastily, almost tripping on her gown. "Yes, but—"

"Is that the only reason you're marrying him?"

"Y–yes."

"Why that. . .that. . ." He started toward the door.

"Wait." Amy put her hands against his chest. "Please, try to calm down."

"Calm down? Just wait 'til I get my hands on that young rapscallion." He stepped sideways, and her hands slid from his chest.

She grabbed his arm. "Father, wait."

He stopped, impatience in every line of his face.

"Please don't do anything rash, Father. You've always told me to think things through completely before making a decision. This house means so much to you." She held up a hand as he started to speak. "I know you told me you're thinking of selling it, but I think you weren't completely honest with me. You aren't thinking of selling because I'm leaving the house, are you? You're thinking of selling because you can't pay the mortgage. My leaving only makes it easier."

He started to protest.

She interrupted him. "Your honest answer, Father."

His gaze searched hers a moment. Then his shoulders dropped slightly. "You're right. But that doesn't mean—"

"I love you, Father. Walter promised our marriage will pay the mortgage in full, including all back payments. I know this is not the way you would choose to pay this debt, but if you need me to do this, I will do it willingly."

His eyes suddenly teared, and Amy found herself wrapped in his embrace. "You are the most precious thing in my life. I want your happiness more than I want my own. We have wonderful memories in this house, but I can leave the house and take the memories. The thought of you as the wife of a man who would blackmail you into marriage. . .it makes me see purple."

Amy pressed back her own tears.

Her father awkwardly patted her shoulders. "Come on, now. Our guests are waiting. I'm looking forward to telling that worm of a man that there isn't going to be a wedding."

They headed for the door hand in hand.

Pearl met them in the hall. "Amy, Walter is waiting for you in the library. He said there's something you two need to discuss before the ceremony and that you'd understand."

The note. How could she have forgotten he'd agreed to sign the note as paid in full before the ceremony began? "Yes, I understand."

"You are running a bit late," Pearl reminded apologetically.

Mr. Henderson grinned. "Later than you think."

Amy threw her arms around Pearl. "We're not getting married."

Pearl gasped and returned the hug. "That's wonderful!"

"Would you tell Walter I'll be right down?"

"I'll be delighted to tell him. Wish I could be there to see the look on his face when you give him the news." Pearl gave Amy's hand a conspiratorial squeeze before she hurried downstairs.

Amy explained quickly to her father why she and Walter had planned to meet.

Her father shook his head, a glint of a smile in his pale blue eyes. "Pretty smart of you to get him to agree to signing the papers over before the ceremony. If you weren't a woman, you'd make a great businessman."

"What do you want me to tell Walter?"

"I thought we already decided the wedding is off."

"I mean about the papers."

His sigh lifted his chest and strained at his white vest buttons. "I admit it's tempting to allow him to sign off that the note is paid in full before telling him the wedding is off, but it wouldn't be truthful."

Amy gave a small sigh of relief. "No, it wouldn't."

"There's no reason for you to face him now. You can stay in your room until I've spoken with him and dismissed the guests."

Amy took her father's arm and urged him toward the stairway. "I'm going with you." The scent of flowers from the parlor below enwrapped them.

"No need for you to be there. This is between us men."

"I'm the one who almost married him. I'm the one who is breaking a promise."

"A promise obtained through deceit," he reminded her in a vigorous whisper, obviously aware of the guests in the parlor.

"A promise just the same." She spoke for his ears alone. "It's only honorable that I face him with the withdrawal of that promise. And you are the one who taught me about honor, after all."

"All right," he agreed with a grudging tone. "But if things get ugly, I expect you to leave."

"Oh, I think it very likely things will get ugly." She avoided agreeing to his request. Happiness bubbled up in her until she felt giddy with it. "Things have been ugly since Walter demanded I marry him."

Amy glimpsed the wedding parlor through the doorway as they passed it on the way to the library. A lace-covered table set along one wall glimmered with crystal and silver wedding gifts. Sobering guilt quieted her runaway emotions. Friends and relatives had sent the gifts as a way to rejoice with Amy and Walter in what they believed was the couple's joy in finding each other. She'd return all of the gifts, of course.

There would be questions about the dissolving of the engagement at such a late hour: questions asked point-blank by the bold, left unspoken by the discreet. Amy would share the truth with no one but Pearl and Frank, but the questions spoken and unspoken would be hard to face.

In the library the desk lamp banished the early evening darkness with a mellow glow cast through the umber globe and lent a deceptively peaceful atmosphere to the room. The fireplace, which warmed the room when her father used it as his office, held only logs ready to light, and the air was chill.

Walter leaned against the desk, watching the door. He looked more commanding than usual, Amy thought, in his black cutaway wedding suit and black patent shoes. His hair was parted fashionably in the middle and the light brown waves so oiled that they glimmered in the lamplight. The proper black cane rested beside him. His cloth wedding gloves fit his hands like soft skin. He held the papers. Amy could hear the quiet slap as he idly bounced them against one palm.

Walter's eyes widened in surprise at the sight of Mr. Henderson with Amy. She saw the question in his eyes, but he said nothing as she and her father came around the desk. Her father sat down in his desk chair. Amy stood beside him, one hand resting on the tall leather chair back.

Together they'd face the enemy, she thought, restraining a giggle.

Walter obviously didn't see anything amusing in the situation. "The wedding should have started fifteen minutes ago. Our guests are getting impatient. Let's get this business over." He opened the papers and laid them on the desk, then began to open the gold-covered ink bottle. "I thought Amy planned to give you the executed agreement after the ceremony, Sir, but I guess this will do just as well. I asked Mrs. Sterling to ꓤ Rev. Conrad in. I suggest we ask him to keep the agreement for safekeeping until the vows are said, as we originally planned, Amy."

Mr. Henderson picked up the papers. "That won't be necessary."

Walter's gaze darted to Amy's. Suspicion darkened his eyes. "What's going on?"

She pressed her lips together tightly. She'd leave this in her father's hands. She sent up a silent prayer asking her heavenly Father to give her earthly father wisdom and restraint.

A quiet knock sounded at the door and Rev. Conrad entered. He stopped just inside the room and stared at the group about the desk, looking unaccustomedly uncertain.

Is the tension in the air so strong he can sense it? Amy glanced at her father. Would he ask Rev. Conrad to leave? Surely he didn't need to safeguard the document now.

Mr. Henderson nodded at the pastor, then turned his attention back to Walter, handing him the folded paper. "You won't need to sign this. My daughter isn't for sale. Not at any price."

Walter's jaw dropped. He accepted the note without seeming to realize it was in his hand. "What—?"

Amy dared a glance at her father out of the corner of her eye.

His gentlemanly voice had been steady and calm, but his eyes glittered with anger. Her hand tightened on the chair back.

Mr. Henderson smiled thinly at the pastor. "Reverend, would you explain to our guests that the bride and groom have changed their minds?"

The slender, bearded pastor was the most reserved man Amy knew. His usually passive face registered shock, but he said nothing. She suspected the pastor knew of other marriages that had been called off at the last minute but expected he hadn't heard the intended groom accused of purchasing his intended bride before.

"Wait." Walter held up a palm toward the pastor, but his glaring eyes were upon Mr. Henderson.

Amy caught her breath.

"There's still time to change your mind, Amy," Walter said, still looking at her father. "I assure you I am going to collect on this note, one way or another." He held the note out.

Mr. Henderson ignored it. "I suggest you collect in the normal business way, Mr. Bay. Now I have a choice for you to make. You may leave the house now, before the guests are dismissed, or you may wait for their condolences."

Walter, his face mottled with anger, stuffed the papers beneath his cutaway jacket. He grabbed his silk top hat from the corner of the desk. With a jerky movement, he picked up his black cane.

The shift in his expression was so swift Amy barely caught it before he struck out with the cane, swiping it across the desktop.

Leather desk blotter, stationery, paperweight, books, inkwell, and pen flew.

Her own screams mingled with those of her father and Rev. Conrad.

Her father leaped back.

Amy lunged toward the lamp, catching it as it teetered after a book clipped the edge of the lamp's base.

"I'll be back." Walter stalked toward the door, settling his top hat on his head as though nothing were abnormal.

"Wait," Amy called. She set the lamp back on the desk, noticing blue ink blotched one lace sleeve.

Walter turned around and waited, hands on his black walking stick in such a normal gentlemanly stance that a sense of the bizarre flashed through her.

She lifted her gown slightly while picking her steps through the mess he'd caused on the floor. When she reached him, his lips stretched in a thin smile. "Change your mind?"

"I only wanted to return this." She pulled the hated emerald from her finger and held it out.

His hands tightened on the top of the walking stick. The thought flashed through her mind that he might again use it as a weapon, this time against her. The knowledge left her trembling, but she resisted the urge to step backward.

Rev. Conrad moved quickly but quietly beside them. He took the ring from her and held it toward Walter. "I think this is best, Mr. Bay, don't you?"

Only respect was evident in his voice, and Amy wondered how he managed it.

Walter hesitated a moment longer, then snatched the ring, stuffed it into a pocket, turned, and left.

"I'll never wear emeralds again," Amy said fiercely. She turned to the pastor. "Thank you." She knew he'd stood beside her, hoping to protect her if Walter lashed out at her with the walking stick.

The crashing of the front door as it was slammed shut reverberated in the house. Amy wondered whether her guests were stretching their necks to see who had been so improper.

"It appears you chose wisely in ending the engagement," Rev. Conrad said quietly. "I'm sure I don't need to tell either of you that I won't repeat what I've witnessed here."

This time Amy's father joined her in thanking the pastor.

"Would you still like me to dismiss the guests?" the pastor asked.

Mr. Henderson grinned. "I'd like that pleasure for myself."

Amy laughed. "I know it's not possible, but it would be nice if the guests could stay. Mrs. Jorgenson and Lina are prepared to serve refreshments. I've more to celebrate now than I did before the wedding was cancelled. Of course, we'd never live down the notoriety."

Her father joined in the laugh, and even the serious pastor smiled.

"We do have a lot of food," Mr. Henderson agreed. "Perhaps it wouldn't be too indiscreet to ask the Reverend here and his wife to stay and join us in enjoying some of it." He raised thick white eyebrows in question.

Rev. Conrad smiled. "Mrs. Conrad and I gladly accept your invitation."

"Perhaps we can ask Pearl and Jason," Amy added. She knew Pearl and Jason would join in her spirit of celebration, even if in silence: celebration of freedom from Walter and, more important, celebration of the chance for her and Frank to discover whether their love was as real as they believed.

&

Amy must be married by now. Frank didn't have a pocket watch in the barn with him, and the evening seemed especially long with the knowledge of Amy's wedding taking place, but surely the vows must have been spoken by now. The thought burned Frank's heart.

He set the T-stool into the straw beside Sudsy. Sitting down, Frank leaned against her warm side with a sigh. "Hi, Sudsy, girl. Did you have a long day, too?" Patient Sudsy was as usual the last cow to be milked. Gideon and two of his female friends took up spots nearby, close enough to be available for a sampling of milk, yet far enough away not to be kicked by Sudsy's hooves.

The milking took longer than usual since Frank was doing it alone. Jason and Pearl were at the wedding. Frank's younger brother and sisters had been invited to Pearl's parents for dinner and to spend the evening. Frank was glad for the solitude. He hadn't the energy or desire to be around anyone. The barn with its familiar smells and the animals he loved was the most comforting place for him.

Gideon jumped onto his knee, stood on his hind legs, and burrowed his head beneath Frank's chin. "Need a hug, Gideon?" The cat always liked to snuggle. "Or do you think I'm the one who needs a hug?" Frank stopped milking to pet the cat. "Maybe both of us need a bit of loving." He hated to admit to himself how much that cat's show of affection meant to him.

Sudsy turned her head to see why Frank had stopped milking and protested noisily. Frank chuckled. Gideon's balancing act was hard to milk around. Frank set him on the ground with reluctance. "Sudsy's going to be mighty upset if I don't finish milking her soon."

He went back to business, gratitude warming his chest. What would he do without these animals? "Wonder how Amy's going to manage without her painting." He imagined that would be as awful for her as life for him without his animal friends.

"Maybe it wouldn't be so bad losing Amy to Walter if he loved her." Gideon responded with a meow and a rub against his legs.

What kind of a bleak, miserable life was ahead for his fine, sweet Amy?

He snorted. "She's not mine."

Gideon leaped to his shoulder and settled there, purring loudly in his ear. Frank gave him an absentminded pat and went back to the milking.

Was he ever going to stop hurting?

A drink would make things better. The familiar thought flowed into his mind as it always did when everything looked bleak and hard and hopeless. He turned from it in the way that was becoming habitual. He knew it would come back and he'd need to push it out of his mind again. He was beginning to think it was going to be like the milking; you did it over and over again, day after day, for the rest of your life.

He'd been so excited when Amy had promised that she'd allow him to court her if he stayed sober for a year. What good was his commitment to the Lord anyway, when people like Walter Bay could ruin his life and Amy's? He'd committed his life to the Lord, given up drinking and gambling, and trusted God to show him and Amy a way out of this situation with Walter. As far as he could see, God wasn't honoring their commitment to Him at all.

That's not true. It's only frustration talking.

He hadn't asked any promises of God when he'd decided to follow Him. God hadn't promised him Amy would love him. God wasn't forcing Amy to marry Walter; that was Amy's choice. A misguided choice from Frank's viewpoint. It was a coward's way out to blame God because life wasn't turning out all peaches and cream.

Jacob hadn't hid from life when he found he'd been deceived by his father-in-law into marrying the wrong woman after seven years. He'd just buckled down and worked another seven years.

"Won't do me any good to wait another seven years for Amy. She's Walter's wife by now and lost to me forever."

Maybe one day God would bring another woman into his life he could love, though he doubted it.

He hoped Amy wouldn't regret every day of her life that she'd married Walter. Frank had told Amy that he'd learned to trust that God had a bigger plan than he could see when life was hard. Maybe living with Amy would change Walter, make a better man of him. Was that God's plan in what seemed a horrid mess?

"Help her, Lord. Somehow please make this marriage turn into something good for her," he whispered.

The barn door creaked. Frank's heart plummeted. The others must be home. He hadn't expected them so soon. Or maybe it was later than he thought. "I'm over here," he called out. "Just finished the milking."

"Down you go," he said, lifting Gideon from his shoulder. "Time to do the separating." He'd tell Jason he'd be glad to finish up himself, gain a little more time alone. He patted Sudsy and pulled the pail of warm milk from beneath her. Boots crunched in the straw, carrying Jason closer.

Frank stood, pail in one hand and T-stool in the other, and turned to greet him. Shock barreled through him. He stared in disbelief at Walter in his silk top hat, fancy full-length overcoat, and shiny dress shoes. His walking stick made a hollow staccato sound as he bounced it against the barn floor. He seemed an apparition, he was so out of place in a barn. Had he come to gloat? "Walter! What are you doing here?"

"As if you don't know."

"Know what?" Frank looked over Walter's shoulder into the darkness of the barn. "Did you come alone?"

"Did you think I'd bring Amy?" Walter's lips twisted in a sneer. "Think I'd be so obliging as to bring her to you?"

"Bring her to me?" Frank felt awash in confusion. Excitement began to stir. He didn't know what was going on, but one thing was certain. Walter wasn't with Amy. "Shouldn't you be celebrating with Amy and your wedding guests about now?"

Walter shoved one of Frank's shoulders. "Stop testing me!"

Milk sloshed over Frank's legs and into his boots as he stumbled backward. "Hey!" Gideon and his companions darted away, out of reach of human feet.

"I know you're behind this," Walter raged. "If you didn't want Amy for yourself, her father would never have found out about my agreement with Amy. She loved him too much. She'd never have let him know she was marrying me to save his precious house." He shoved Frank again.

Frank stumbled into Sudsy. Trying to avoid her hooves and

not hurt her with the stool, he sidestepped, barely regaining his balance.

Walter pushed at him once more, but this time his hand glanced off Frank's shoulder.

Frank dropped the stool and pail into the straw that hindered him and lifted his arms to defend himself. He didn't want to fight; he wanted to find out what had happened between Walter and Amy. Apparently the wedding hadn't taken place, but he didn't dare hope that was the truth. "I didn't say anything to Mr. Henderson."

Walter gave a short bark of a laugh. "You think Amy would?"

"No, of course not." Frank tried to work himself away from Sudsy and the other cows. If Walter insisted on a fight, Frank didn't want to land beneath any hooves or somehow harm the cows.

He'd told the truth. He didn't think Amy would tell her father the reason she was marrying Walter. He'd sure tried to convince her to often enough. "What did her father say?"

"What do you think he said? He called off the wedding."

Joy washed through Frank. "He did?"

Walter growled and slashed out with his stick.

Frank leaped back. The stick missed its mark. His heart was racing now.

Walter swung again.

Frank grabbed the stick and flung it away into the darkness. He heard the soft plop when it landed in the straw.

He didn't like the way the cows were getting restless. They were grumbling their protests, shifting about. They'd moved away from the lantern that hung on the post where he'd been milking. The light's rays were dim in this part of the barn. No telling what they might fall over or step in. "If you want to fight, let's go outside."

Walter tripped over a T-stool and swore. Picking up the stool, he tossed it at Frank.

He dodged. It struck his arm. He grunted and winced from

the blow but kept moving toward the barn door, walking backward so he could keep an eye on Walter. He bumped into a post. Darted a glance over his shoulder and adjusted his path. Looked back at Walter.

Walter's body blocked Frank's view of the lantern, but Frank saw its light glint off something in Walter's hands. The pitchfork!

He glued his gaze to the tool-turned-weapon. Fear tunneled up his backbone and prickled his hair. He reached toward heaven with a wordless prayer, feeling his way backward with his work boots.

"Walter, you don't want to do this. You can marry most any woman you want." The straw crackled beneath his boots.

"You think this is just about Amy?"

Frank's gaze flicked to Walter's face and back to the fork. "It's about the money? You still hold the note on Amy's father's house. You're one of the most successful men in town and half the age of most of the businessmen."

"It's not Amy, and it's not the money."

"What then?" Frank's arms swung wide in frustration.

Walter lunged.

Frank dove to the side.

The tines of the pitchfork caught Frank's open jacket and drove into the wood of a stall.

Walter chuckled. "You're about as harmless as a pinned butterfly." He leaned into the fork's handle. "It isn't about Amy or money, Sterling. It's about power. It's all about power."

The quiet way he spoke caused fear to burn like a white-hot coal in Frank's stomach.

Walter pulled on the pitchfork. He couldn't get it unstuck. He tugged, lost his balance, and fell back into the straw, striking his head on the other side of the stall.

Sweat dampened Frank's hands as he jerked one arm out of its sleeve and worked on releasing the other, watching Walter all the time.

Walter rubbed his head, swearing. His arm bumped something leaning against the stall, and he turned his head to see what it was. He stood and picked up the shovel from beside him.

Desperation sickened Frank. He wrenched his arm free at last. The suddenness unbalanced him. He heard the shovel *whoosh* as Walter swung it. Then something slammed against the side of his head. The last thing he heard was the straw crackling against his head.

He wasn't sure how much later something small and damp and scratchy against his eyelid awakened him. He turned his head. Pain crashed through his skull, and he gasped.

The rhythmic scratchiness started again against his eyelid. He tried to reach to brush it away. It took all his strength. The heaviness of his arm, the slowness with which it moved, seemed like part of a bad dream. His hand touched something warm and furry. "Gideon," he whispered—or tried to.

The straw-covered floor beneath him vibrated. He tried to think what could cause such a thing. It was the cows, he realized. The cows were bellowing. It sounded like they were trying to get away from something. Curiosity grew in him. He started to open his eyes, but that made his already aching head feel like someone was taking a hatchet to it.

"Meow. Meo–o–o–ow." Gideon bumped his head against Frank's chin.

The cat was sure being insistent.

The odors of straw and dirt and animals mingled with something that shouldn't be there. Something scary. Something that hurt his nose and throat and eyes.

Smoke!

eighteen

Amy closed the door behind the last of their departing guests. She slipped her hand beneath her father's arm, and he patted her hand as they walked slowly toward the parlor.

The room had already resumed much of its everyday air. While Amy'd been upstairs changing from her ink-splattered wedding gown into a simple white shirtwaist and black skirt, the parlor had also undergone a transformation. Her father, Rev. and Mrs. Conrad, Jason, Lina, and Mrs. Jorgenson had removed the gifts and the large satin bows that had decorated the room, as well as many of the flowers. Most of the food had been removed from the dining room to the kitchen, including the cake over which Mrs. Jorgenson had labored so many hours. Gratitude for her father's and friends' thoughtfulness warmed Amy.

A couple large bouquets remained and perfumed the air, but Amy didn't mind.

Mr. Henderson sat down on the sofa. He'd removed his black cutaway coat and white vest and collar. He looked comfortably homey in his white shirt with the top button open.

Amy settled beside him, facing him. "I'm glad the Conrads and Sterlings stayed for coffee, Father. Visiting with them washed away some of the. . .awfulness of the evening. I'm not certain awfulness is a word, but I can't think of another that adequately describes the horror I feel whenever I realize how close I came to marrying Walter." A shiver ran through her at the thought.

Her father grunted in agreement. "It's enough to give a man apoplexy."

Amy's laugh rang out. It felt so good to laugh freely and easily again.

"It's the truth," Mr. Henderson insisted. "To think I urged you to see Walter, to give him a chance to court you. I should have trusted your instincts about men."

"A compliment like that could go to a girl's head."

"Tease me if you must. I deserve it."

Amy's soft chuckle died. "All my instincts weren't wise. It's true I've never trusted Walter, though I didn't have a specific reason not to at first. My instincts on how to handle his threats against you weren't sound.

"I lost count of how many times I asked God to show me what to do. I kept wondering whether Walter was a Christian. I knew it couldn't be God's will to marry Walter if we didn't share a love for Christ. I'm ashamed to admit I refused to face the issue. I knew if I did, I'd have to tell Walter I wouldn't marry him, and I'd have to tell you everything, and you'd lose the house. I see now that telling you everything was what God wanted me to do. My doubts about Walter's faith were the answer to my prayer for guidance."

"Your actions came from love. I hate that Walter used your love for me against you, terrorized you that way, and blackmailed you into agreeing to marry him. I hate that he played my friend while planning behind my back to steal you away." His round cheeks grew ruddy. "Most of all, I hate that you believed I loved this house and money and my pride more than I loved you."

"But I don't." Amy leaned toward him and rested one of her hands on his arm. "You don't understand. I didn't tell you about Walter's blackmail because I knew you loved me too much to allow me to marry him to save you."

He patted her hand, his eyes damp with tears. "I'm glad you told me before it was too late."

She still didn't like to think of him losing respect in the

eyes of the townspeople and other businessmen, but Frank was right: Her father's life was his own to lead. "Frank convinced me to tell you."

"Sterling?" His white brows rose in surprise. "Wanted you for himself, I suppose."

"I hope so." Her lips quirked in a mischievous smile. "Seriously, he said I should show you the respect of allowing you to make your own decisions about your life."

"I'll make sure to thank him." He sighed. "Another man I misjudged, it seems."

"Frank is a good man, Father. He's kind and compassionate and strong and wise and—"

His laugh bounded out. "Sounds like you're more than a little fond of him."

She felt herself blushing. Her fingers played with the locket she'd moved from the wedding gown to her blouse. "I am."

"Expect he'll be coming around now that Walter's out of the way."

"I expect." Joy danced in her heart at the prospect. "Where do you suppose that will be?"

Her father frowned. "Where will what be?"

Amy sobered. "Us. What will we do now? Walter will take the house, won't he?" It was more a statement than a question.

"Yes, I'm sure he will. Another man might have given me warning, allowed me time to sell the house and try to regain enough money to pay off the loan, but not Walter."

"Frank offered a solution. He asked me to marry him. We'd live at the Sterling farm, and you would be welcome to live there with us."

Her father swallowed hard before replying. "I appreciate his offer, but I'm not about to allow you to marry another man just to put a roof over our heads."

She twisted the locket and smiled. "I wouldn't marry Frank just to put a roof over our heads."

"You and young Sterling need to court properly for awhile before you marry. From the way you speak of him, he sounds like as fine a man as I could want for you. But you need to discover if what you feel for each other is truly love or only admiration blown out of proportion by the separation I forced on you this last year. Besides, Frank's still attending school. Didn't you tell me he wants to attend the university in St. Paul, too?"

"Yes, to take the agricultural course there."

"Don't you still want to visit Paris?"

"Paris will wait for me." That dream seemed unattainable, considering her father's financial state. She didn't imagine Frank would have enough money for them to travel to Paris. Even if he did, she doubted the farmer was interested in dawdling around the city while she visited the Louvre and tried to obtain audiences with the famous painters in France.

"All the same, I think it's time I found some paying work instead of waiting around for my investments to regain their health. Things might look bleak, but I'll find a place for us. It won't be fancy like this, but I promise you a roof over our heads."

Amy rested her head on his shoulder. "I've no doubt you'll keep that promise."

Funny how peace fills me now, she thought, *when it looks like we're going to be penniless.* "We have each other and God. We're going to be fine."

❧

Heading back to the farm from Chippewa City, the runners on the Sterlings' wagon sang over the prairie snow. *Sh-sh-sh-sh.* The wagon rode smooth, rocking and sliding over the snow-covered road. It was a treat compared to the rough rides over the rutted summer road.

Frank and Jason's younger siblings snuggled beneath lap robes on top of the hay in the wagon bed. Pearl's mother had warmed bricks for the ride home. An invigorating chill against their cheeks encouraged the Sterlings to keep the robes pulled up to their chins.

They sang into the night, silly ditties that reflected the fun of a night free from the farm for the youngsters. Sleigh bells jangled on the two horses in accompaniment to the voices. For Jason and Pearl the songs were a release from the tension of a day that had started with dread of Amy's wedding but ended in joy.

"I love the prairie sky on winter nights." Pearl snuggled close to Jason on the wagon seat. They shared the thick buffalo robe. Their feet rested on two warmed bricks. The children's singing allowed her conversation with Jason to feel private. The moon reflecting off the snow brightened the night until lanterns weren't needed. Distant lights could be seen from farmhouse windows scattered across the prairie. The air was crisp, occasionally warmed by wood smoke or coal smoke from a nearby farm. "Do you remember what Byron calls the stars? 'The poetry of heaven.'"

Jason chuckled. "No, can't say I remember, not being a reader of poetry."

"I like you anyway."

"I should hope so, since you're stuck with me."

Pearl rubbed her head against Jason's shoulder. "I'm glad Amy isn't stuck with Walter."

"Amen," he agreed fervently. "I've been mighty worried about Frank since Amy became engaged to Bay. Frank was hurting something fierce. I wonder whether Amy and Frank will begin courting now that Bay's out of the way. I know Frank's crazy about her, but do you think she likes him? I mean, as much as he likes her?"

"Oh, yes." Pearl smiled, remembering Amy's painting of Frank. Pearl wasn't delivering the painting to Frank after all. There was no need since the wedding didn't take place. "I'm so glad for both of them. I remember how awful it was when

I didn't know whether you loved me."

He winked at her. "And how wonderful it was when we discovered we loved each other."

"It's still wonderful."

Jason took one hand from the reins and reached across her lap, making sure the buffalo robe was tucked firmly about her. "Are you and our little one warm enough?"

She nodded. His concern for them warmed her more than the robe.

He slid his arm around her shoulder, squeezed her gently close, and whispered in her ear, "Just think. Before next Christmas we'll know that little tyke face-to-face. Can't wait to hold that baby."

Pearl laughed, patting her stomach lightly. "You haven't much choice, Sir."

He drew his arm back. Pearl wished he'd left it but knew he didn't feel safe driving one-handed. One never knew when the horses would take a fright from a strange shadow or unexpected noise or a wild creature darting out of a ditch. It seemed to her the horses were acting a bit skittish now, though she couldn't see a reason. They were tossing their heads slightly and nickering in a nervous manner.

She glanced at Jason. Worry lined his face.

"What is it, Jason?"

"I don't know. Do you have a good hold? I don't want you slipping off the seat if they balk."

She gripped the edge of the seat, but her mittened grip didn't feel as secure as she'd like. She reminded herself that Jason was strong and a good driver. What was causing the horses' fright? Was there a wolf or other predator hiding out here somewhere? There wasn't much place for anything to hide. The snow revealed every shadow. The only trees were those around farmsteads.

The wagon lost its smooth journey as the horses' pace

grew jerkier. The kids stopped their singing; first fourteen-year-old Andy, then thirteen-year-old Maggie, and finally six-year-old Grace. Andy's head popped up over the seat back. "What's going on?"

"Not sure." Jason clipped his words. "Get back down, and see the girls stay down, too."

Andy obeyed immediately.

They'd almost reached the drive leading to their farm. Pearl could see the row of poplars that lined the long drive from the road to the yard. Blue shadows cast by the trees stretched across the snow.

"Almost home." Relief underscored Jason's observation.

Something tugged at Pearl's brain. Something wasn't right, but she couldn't place her finger on it. Something about the air, but what? There wasn't anything unusual in it: the cold, the hay from the wagon bed, the strong scent of the buffalo robe, smoke from their farmstead—but Frank was home so the stoves should be lit.

"Jason, the smoke. It smells stronger than usual to me."

Jason's glance met hers for a moment. She saw the concern in his eyes, but he said nothing.

He pulled on the reins. "Who–o–a. Slow down, boys. Time to turn." The horses followed the leading of the reins and turned onto the drive.

They'd only traveled a third of the way when Pearl saw it. It was only a flash at first, but she knew. Fear rippled down her spine. "The barn, Jason. The barn's on fire."

He took it in with one glance. "Move!" He slapped the reins, leaned forward, urging the horses on. "Hold on!"

Pearl held on. She grabbed the top of the footboard with both hands, trusting her grasp there better than on the seat. She heard Grace begin to cry. Pearl's gaze stayed on the barn. Only a narrow streak of flame flared out. The barn wasn't engulfed. If it were, they'd have seen it. Fire couldn't hide on a moonlit, snow-covered prairie.

The crackling of the fire and cries of frightened animals filled the air as they neared the yard. The two farm dogs barked wildly, racing alongside the wagon. Jason slowed the horses to a stop and threw the reins to Pearl. "Tie them. Maggie, Grace, get some buckets from the kitchen. Come with me, Andy." He leaped down from the wagon and started at a run. "Frank must be in the barn."

Frank and the animals, Pearl realized as she and the others followed Jason's directives. Her mind raced. What had happened? How had it started? Why hadn't Frank released any of the farm animals? Was he in the barn? In the house? Had he gone into town? Had he been so downhearted over Amy's marriage that he'd finally given in and started drinking?

She ran onto the porch, almost slipping on the wooden steps. She grabbed an iron bar and swung it in a circle again and again, ringing the triangle used to call the men from the fields. Its noise battered her ears. Was the clanging loud enough to catch their neighbors' attention?

Maggie and Grace stumbled past her toward the well, the buckets making it difficult for them to run.

Pearl tore toward the barn. She had to help the men get the animals out. Where was Frank? *Dear God, help us!*

nineteen

Smoke!

The realization seeped into Frank's brain. The smoke meant fire. The cows' and horses' terrorized screams tore at his heart. He struggled to rise, pushing against the floor with his arms. They bent like prairie grass before a storm. *Help me, God, please.*

He kept trying. If he didn't get out, he'd never see Amy again. He rolled against the stall wall and managed with great effort to little by little sit up against it. *I have to get to Sudsy. Have to get the animals out. It's only You and me, God.* The smoke burned his eyes and nose. His head pounded worse with every movement. His eyes blurred.

But his arms and legs were getting stronger. The shovel Walter had wielded against him was lying beside him. Using it to lever himself, Frank pushed and pulled himself to a standing position.

He half dragged the shovel with him, half leaned on it for support as he moved toward Sudsy. The fire seemed nearer her than the other animals. He couldn't be sure. His vision doubled and tripled images. The fire licking along the outer wall supplied light so he could tell where to go. The flames would feed rapidly on the straw. Every moment counted, and a tortoise could move faster than he could.

He was almost there. "It's all right, Sudsy." He laid a hand on her flank.

She lurched.

Frank lost his balance and started falling.

"Frank!"

Was that Jason? Frank wondered as he landed on the floor. The jolt caused an eruption of stars in his head. With an effort, he tried to roll away from Sudsy's hooves.

Then Jason was kneeling beside him, tugging beneath his arms, dragging him into a sitting position. "Frank, are you all right? Can you stand?"

"Need a little help." Why did his words slur together that way? "Sudsy. . .the cows. . ."

"Andy will get Sudsy. Let's get you outside."

Frank felt one of his arms pulled over Jason's shoulder, and then Jason lifted him to his feet. He tried to walk, but Jason moved too fast.

A blast of cold air hit them.

"Pearl, hold the door," Jason demanded.

She gasped. "Is Frank all right?"

"I'm not sure," Jason said as they moved past her into the outdoors. "Get out of here."

"I'll help Andy with the animals."

"No!"

She disappeared into the barn. Didn't surprise Frank. Pearl was that kind of person.

Frank drank in the cold air. "I'm all right." He pulled his arm from his brother's shoulder. He tried to steady himself, but he swayed despite his best effort. "Get the animals out."

"Frank—"

He could see the indecision and anguish on Jason's face. "Get them out!"

Jason grimaced and turned back to the barn.

Andy was leading Sudsy and another cow through the door.

"Thank God." Frank sank into the snow. He hadn't the strength to go back into the barn. Would the others be able to get the animals out in time?

A shadow caught his attention. Their neighbors, Thor and his wife, Ellie, were rushing into the yard. Gratitude rushed over Frank in a wave. If Thor had seen the fire, maybe other neighbors had as well.

"Meo—o—o—ow." Gideon stood on his hind legs and looked into Frank's face.

Frank ran a hand along the thin, fur-covered back. "I'll be all right, Gideon, thanks to you. Here I thought you were a cat, and all along God knew you were an angel."

Ellie knelt beside him. "What are you doing out here with no coat? And what happened to your head? It's bleeding."

"It is?" He lifted a hand to the place that pounded. Sticky. "Guess the fire caught my attention."

Frank allowed her to help him toward the house. More neighbors were entering the yard as they crossed it, some on snowshoes, some on horseback, some in a wagon on runners. Animals freed from the barn were rushing about the yard. People called to each other and the animals. The fire snapped and popped and made its own wind. A haze of smoke dulled the star-sprinkled sky. Cinders drifted down like misshapen, dirty snowflakes.

Frank turned his back on the melee. Guilt tugged at him, but he knew he'd be more hindrance than help.

Ellie helped him to the green plush sofa in the parlor, then found a cold wet cloth for his head before returning to the yard.

Frank lay on the sofa, the cloth pressed to his head, and stared out the window for a long while, watching the flames leap and listening to the frantic sounds. He prayed for his family and friends and for the animals.

And he prayed for Amy. Thank God she'd escaped marriage to Walter. What happened to change everything? What had her father found out, and how?

Finally he could fight the pain and exhaustion no longer, and he slipped into sleep.

He was awakened an hour later by Pearl's father, Dr. Matt Strong. The doctor cleaned Frank's head wound, bandaged it, gave him some headache powders, and told him to stay awake for awhile. "Your blurred vision worries me. Could have a concussion."

"I'm not seeing double anymore."

"Just the same, stay awake."

"Guess I'll have some of that coffee I smell. One of the ladies must be brewing it for the people fighting the fire."

"You have a lot of good neighbors out there."

"We sure do." Frank touched his bandaged head gingerly. "How did you hear I needed you?"

"Jason sent one of the neighbors for me."

"Glad he did." Flames still brightened the world outside the window. "How are things going out there?"

"As you can see, the barn's still burning. Afraid that will be a total loss. Jason thinks all the animals were saved, though."

Frank rested his head against the tidy-covered sofa back. "Thank the Lord." He felt suddenly relaxed. He hadn't realized his muscles had tightened like a spring against what he might hear.

Dr. Matt patted Frank's knee. "I'll get you that coffee."

It was a long night. The Chippewa City volunteer fire department joined the farmers in fighting the fire, but by morning the barn was a smoldering mass of burned timbers in a puddle of melted snow. Silos and the grain that had filled them lay in ashes also. Smoke was thick in the yard and even in the house, though the house had escaped the flames.

Neighbor women filled the kitchen, serving a breakfast of sausage, potatoes, toast, pie, and coffee in shifts to the men. The Sterlings' friends, who had spent the night fighting for them, continued to work, gathering up the animals and taking them home to their own barns until the Sterlings could make other arrangements.

Frank joked, "It will be interesting going visiting to do the milking. Should we wear our dress suits and take our calling cards?"

The crowd of soot-covered, weary neighbors at the breakfast table chuckled politely. "Don't you boys worry none about milking today," one of the farmers ordered. "We'll all take care of the cows boarding in our barns."

The assistance wasn't a joke. It was beyond the power of humans to repay such kindness. The Sterlings thanked each of their friends with quiet, simple words of gratitude straight from their hearts. It was accepted with self-conscious shrugs or nods and averted looks and mumbles that the Sterlings would do the same for them if the need arose and "there but for the grace of God. . . ."

Dawn brought exhaustion, curious townspeople, and the Hendersons.

Frank's gaze hungrily sought Amy's. He had a dozen questions to ask, and questions filled her eyes, too. There was no privacy in which to ask them with the house full of people.

"Are you all right?" she asked, looking at the bandage on Frank's head when they had a moment beside each other.

"I'm tired, dizzy, and my head pounds like a blacksmith beating on an anvil, but Dr. Matt promises I'll recover." Even the pain lightened now that she was with him.

The neighbors and firefighters from town drifted out. A few ladies remained to help clean up in the kitchen. The Sterlings, the Hendersons, and Dr. Matt retired to the parlor and closed the door. The family hadn't had a chance to discuss the night's events, and though their bodies ached for their beds, their hearts needed answers. Only six-year-old Grace gave in and slept.

Frank took hold of Amy's hand and drew her down beside him on the sofa. A rosy glow colored her cheeks, but she allowed him to keep her hand in his. The simple trust he felt from her put a glow around his heart. Last night in the barn he'd thought he might never see her again. The need to touch her now was irresistible. He saw from their glances that the others in the room noticed his and Amy's connection, though no one commented on it.

Jason led out with the question most on everyone's mind. "What happened last night, Frank? How did the fire start?"

Frank shrugged. "I don't know. I have some suspicions, but I don't know for sure."

Jason grimaced. "I had some suspicions, too, when I found you in the barn last night unable to stand and slurring your words."

Frank felt the startled glances of the others on him. Amy's fingers tightened about his. Was she telling him she trusted him, even now?

"I owe you an apology," Jason said. "It was your head wound that was the problem. At first I thought you'd been drinking and hurt yourself when you fell. Then I found this." He held up Frank's chore jacket. "I couldn't think of any reason you'd take it off on a winter night and attach it to a stall with a pitchfork."

A collective gasp filled the room.

Frank patted Amy's hand, hoping to reassure her.

"Why don't you tell us what happened, Frank?" Jason suggested. "As much as you can recall, from the beginning."

So he did. He started with Walter's arrival while he was milking Sudsy, through the attack, to Gideon's gentle yet insistent awakening.

The cat's loyalty earned laughter, which relieved some of the tension Frank's story had built within the family.

"I'll never belittle your pet names again," Jason promised. Addressing Amy, he added, "The way cats multiply around the farm, no one bothers to name them except Frank. He has a name for every one of them. For that matter, he has a name for every cow and hog."

Amy's radiant smile told the room she approved of Frank's attachment to the animals he cared for.

Her father returned to a more serious topic. "So you don't know whether Walter Bay set the fire?"

Frank shook his head. "No. As I said, I have my suspicions, but I can't prove them. I have questions, too. If Bay did set the fire with the purpose of killing me, why not start it closer to me? Or why not just hit me again with the shovel? I wasn't in any shape to fight back."

He felt Amy's shudder and wished he'd been less graphic.

A horrible thought drained the blood from his face. "Has anyone seen Walter? He couldn't. . . Is it possible. . . ?" He couldn't make himself put it into words. What if Walter had been caught in the fire and no one had looked for him because no one but Frank knew he was there?

He knew from the way the room went completely still that everyone understood what he hadn't said.

Andy gave them all release. "Bay wasn't caught in the fire. One of the first neighbors to show up last night saw him."

A collective sigh of relief went up.

"Are you sure?" Frank asked.

Andy nodded. "The neighbor mentioned it at breakfast. Thought it strange Bay was heading for town when he knew everyone else was headed here to help. Then thought maybe Bay was going to raise the alarm with the fire department."

"I don't think so." Amy's soft voice trembled. "If his intentions were honorable, why didn't he pull Frank out of the barn first and try to save the animals?"

No one had an answer. Horrified glances were exchanged among the group.

A chill settled in Frank's bones. To think sweet Amy almost married that cold-hearted man. He drew her hand beneath his arm and pressed it close.

Jason stood. "Since you're not in any shape to go anywhere

yet, Frank, I think I'd best ride into Chippewa City and tell Sheriff Amundson our suspicions. Bay may have already left town or be getting ready to leave. If he's still in town, he must know Frank isn't dead and will tell about the attack."

"But I have no proof he set the fire." Frank didn't like the idea of accusing Walter without proof, as much as he disliked the man.

"I think we still need to report his actions," Jason argued.

Dr. Matt and Mr. Henderson agreed.

Pearl stood, stifling a yawn. "I think the rest of us should get some sleep."

"I'd like another cup of coffee before I leave," her father said. "I've some stops to make before I head home, and a cup to keep my eyes open would be appreciated."

Mr. Henderson, Amy, and Frank stayed behind when the others left the room. Dr. Matt brought in his cup of coffee and joined them, settling himself in the high-backed oak rocker.

Mr. Henderson sat on the edge of the green overstuffed chair, rubbing his palms together, and cleared his throat. "I owe you an apology, Frank. I offer it now, complete and without reservation."

Surprise lifted Frank's brows. "You owe me an apology? Why?"

Dr. Matt started to rise. "Sounds like I've barged in on a private discussion."

Mr. Henderson waved him back to his seat. "You may as well stay. Not many secrets in a town this size. Besides, you're related to Frank through Pearl, and families have a hard time keeping secrets." He turned back to Frank. "I told Amy awhile back that I didn't want you two courting. I didn't think leopards changed their spots."

Embarrassment surged over Frank. He couldn't look at Amy's father or Dr. Matt, so he looked at his and Amy's joined hands instead.

"Yes, we shall, and I am going to look for a job."

"If you need something until you get back on your feet, I could use someone to manage my drugstore. The apartment over the store will be vacant the end of the month, too."

Mr. Henderson beamed. He walked over to Dr. Matt and held out his hand. "I'd be honored to work with you. And we'd be glad to move into your apartment, wouldn't we, Amy?"

"Yes, definitely."

Frank was pleased she didn't hesitate at all in her response and thrilled at the way the Lord was supplying a way for them.

"We should leave soon, Amy," Mr. Henderson said, "and let Frank get some rest. If Dr. Matt is willing, I'll just have a cup of coffee with him in the kitchen before we go. Talk a little business."

Frank rubbed a hand over his chin, hiding his grin. He was pretty sure the business talk could wait. Mr. Henderson was giving him and Amy some precious minutes alone to say good-bye. . .and hello.

Dr. Matt stood up. "Yes, indeed, another cup of coffee is just the thing. About that foreclosure; maybe I could loan you enough to get you up-to-date on the payments. Would you like to consider it?"

The two men walked out of the parlor, pulling the door shut behind them.

"I feel foolish," Amy said. "I acted so much the martyr, thinking only I could save Father from certain destruction. Since I took your advice and told Father about Walter's blackmail, everything seems to be working out fine for Father."

"You weren't acting foolishly. You acted out of love." Frank shifted to face her. He cradled her face between his hands, touching her as tenderly as he was able. It was a gift to be allowed to touch this precious woman. "I just want to look at you," he whispered, happiness welling up within him. "I was afraid I might never see you again."

"I was wrong." Henderson's voice was firm. "Amy told me so, and she was right."

"Thank you, Sir." Frank supposed he should feel pride. Instead he felt humbled. "I think, though, that you were wise demanding that I prove my change of heart by abstaining from liquor and gambling for a year. I took my decision to change seriously, but I didn't realize when I made it how tough it would be. Then, too, lads are beginning to pay attention to Maggie, though she's only thirteen. I realized I wouldn't want any men who court her to drink."

"I'm glad you understand." Henderson smiled. "I also wish to thank you. Amy told me of your offer to allow me to live with you if you two marry."

Dr. Matt sat up quickly, choking on his coffee.

Amy and Frank exchanged laughing glances.

Mr. Henderson held up an index finger. "On this, Dr. Matt, I would appreciate your discretion." Turning his attention back to Frank, he continued. "Although I'm grateful for your offer, I must decline. You've proven yourself an honorable man, and obviously Amy is willing to accept your attentions. But marriage is a lifetime contract, and I believe a little more courting time is in order for you two before any hard and fast decisions are made regarding matrimony."

"Yes, Sir," Frank agreed. "If it's not too bold to ask, what do you plan to do? About Walter, I mean, and his demands. He does still plan to foreclose on your home, doesn't he?"

Dr. Matt sputtered over his coffee again. "Foreclosure, attempted murder, marriage possibilities. This is rather a lot of serious conversation for this early in the day, don't you think?"

They joined in a hearty laugh.

"To answer your question, Frank," Mr. Henderson responded, "I fully expect Walter to foreclose. I don't know yet what Amy and I will do, but we'll work something out."

"Will you need a place to live?" Dr. Matt asked.

think? We can go sleighing. I can walk you home from classes, carrying your books. This spring we can join the other couples out on the Academy steps in the evenings."

There were other things to discuss, like how they'd manage to send Amy to Paris and how many children they hoped to have one day, but there was plenty of time for that. Now that Walter was out of their lives, there would be time for everything.

"Don't forget ice skating," Amy said, continuing his list of courting activities.

"Hmm. We could do that tonight."

She shook her head, laughing at him again. "Not likely, with that cut on your head." She sobered. "It must hurt horribly. Are you still dizzy?"

"Yes, but I'm not sure if it's from the wound or from your closeness."

"Silly boy," she whispered, surprising and delighting him with a quick kiss.

"I won't be a boy by the time I'm through with school and we can marry."

"I'll wait as long as you ask me to wait. What else is there for me to do? You hold my heart."

The promise in her eyes settled every question he'd ever had about her love. A deep peace filled him. "And you hold my heart, Amy. Forever."

He sealed their promises with a kiss.

A sweet smile gentled her face. "I want to look at you, too. Listening to what happened to you last night—" She shuddered. "You might have died, and that would have been my fault, too."

He laughed softly. "You take way too much responsibility for the things that happen to other people."

"If I hadn't gone along with Walter's perverted plan to begin with, he wouldn't have had any cause to attack you."

"No? I don't think we can understand the way his mind works. Let's forget him for awhile. Let Jason and Sheriff Amundson worry about him."

Her smile returned. "That sounds like a good idea."

"May I kiss you, sweet Amy?"

Her lashes swept low and lifted in a shy, entrancing move that hid, then revealed eyes reflecting his own longing and happiness. "Yes," she whispered and closed her eyes.

He touched his lips softly to hers for the length of a heartbeat. Then again, his hands still framing her face. His lips moved to one eyebrow, and then the other, barely brushing them, then back to her mouth. His arms slid around her, drawing her to him as the kiss lengthened. One of her arms slid about his waist in a slightly hesitant manner, and she rested against him.

When the kiss ended, he brushed his lips back and forth over hers lightly and whispered, "I love you, Amy. I love you with all my heart and soul."

"I love you, too. I thought I'd never have the right to say those words to you."

He buried his face in her neck and held her close, rejoicing in her love. "I wish we could marry now, tonight."

She laughed softly at his fervent tone.

He drew back slightly with a sigh. "I suppose your father's right that we shouldn't marry so soon." He traced her cheekbone with an index finger. "It will be fun courting, don't you